PROTÉGÉ OF A LEGEND

Lock Down Publications and Ca$h Presents

Protégé of a Legend

A Novel by *Corey Robinson*

Lock Down Publications
Po Box 944
Stockbridge, Ga 30281

Visit our website @
www.lockdownpublications.com

First Edition May 2022
Printed in the United States of America

Lock Down Publications
Like our page on Facebook: Lock Down Publications @
www.facebook.com/lockdownpublications.ldp
Book interior design by: **Shawn Walker**

Stay Connected with Us!

Text **LOCKDOWN** to 22828 to stay up-to-date with new releases, sneak peaks, contests and more…
Thank you.

Submission Guideline.

Submit the first three chapters of your completed manuscript to ldpsubmissions@gmail.com, subject line: Your book's title. The manuscript must be in a .doc file and sent as an attachment. Document should be in Times New Roman, double spaced and in size 12 font. Also, provide your synopsis and full contact information. If sending multiple submissions, they must each be in a separate email.

Have a story but no way to send it electronically? You can still submit to LDP/Ca$h Presents. Send in the first three chapters, written or typed, of your completed manuscript to:

LDP: Submissions Dept
Po Box 944
Stockbridge, Ga 30281

DO NOT send original manuscript. Must be a duplicate.

Provide your synopsis and a cover letter containing your full contact information.

Thanks for considering LDP and Ca$h Presents.

Prologue

When I walked in, the courtroom was packed and when I spoke, all eyes were on me.

"It wasn't him. It was me. He's just trying to protect me, but I did it. I'm the one who killed that motherfucker."

The words came out of my mouth before I could stop them. I had to do it because I couldn't let Marcus go to prison. He was a young black man tied to the streets, and they would have given him life for sure. He didn't stand a chance and would end up getting lost in the system.

Me, I was a young white girl in love with the thug on the stand. I would be given a slap on the wrist and told to leave him alone. They would assure me that I could do better, but to me, Marcus was the best.

He was the man my momma and daddy warned me about. The type of man they tried so hard to keep me away from. However, the more I was warned about the forbidden fruit, the more I wanted to taste it and once I took a bite, I had to have more. Marcus was like a shot of heroin to a junkie, and I was like a vein beneath the skin pulsing in need of that shot.

My young mind told me that Marcus would ride the time with me. He would take care of me and be waiting with open arms when I walked out of those gates. He would appreciate me even more than he already did because of the sacrifice I made for him. Marcus loved me. I could feel it and I knew that I wouldn't regret my decision by doing this for him because he would have done the same thing for me…

Wouldn't he?

Chapter One

There I sat once again in the cold and lonely cell. The razor blade held tightly between my small fingers while the tears fell from my soulless eyes. I heard the voices as they echoed in my mental…

"Bitch, you ain't got the guts."

"You's a dumb bitch."

"Go ahead, ho. Don't nobody give a fuck, anyway." "You should do your throat instead, bitch."

I embraced death because I had nothing to live for. I'd lost my momma to cancer when I was seventeen years old, and my daddy less than six months later to a broken heart. Marcus, he may have been walking around breathing, but that bastard was dead to me. I had given him everything. My love, my loyalty, my innocence, and my freedom. All he gave me in return was his ass to kiss. I had spent the last ten years of my life behind prison walls because of him. No, he didn't make me do what I did, but my heart told me that he would ride the time with me. However, as soon as the cuffs were secured around my wrists, that motherfucker was history.

"Madison, put the blade down now," the female officer that stood in front of my cell said in a stern, authoritative voice. She had caught me doing it several times before, but I had told her that next time it would be different. The next time I would really go through with it, and that time had arrived. I'd gripped the blade tighter and then looked up into her concerned eyes. I felt the chills as they climbed my spine before I ever made contact and when my flesh opened, I heard the officer in the background singing a different tune.

"I got a ten-fifteen on the Charlie wing with an attempted suicide. I need medical and all other available staff to assist immediately."

That would teach her to call my bluff. As I lay there barely conscience, I watched the blood flow from the downward slit I had just made. Flashes of my life passed through my blurred vision. That happy little girl with a heart full of love was gone. Replaced by a heartbroken, bitter woman with nothing, but hatred running through her veins. The veins, she had just cut to try to escape the cold, cold world.

There was not one loving soul who would have mourned my death. No one would have even remembered my name because I had long been forgotten. In my whole ten years there, I had never received a letter, not one picture. Not even a flyer asking me to give myself to The Lord. I didn't have any friends because I honestly didn't know how to be one myself.

I was an only child growing up and at school, no one liked me enough to even talk to me. That was why I fell so hard for Marcus. He made me feel special and worthy. He picked me up from the downward spiral my life had taken and made me feel like I belonged. He made me feel important and needed, which was why I couldn't understand why he never reached out to me. What did I do to deserve this?

I still remembered the last words he spoke as I was escorted out of the courtroom. I heard them as plain as day. It was as if he was standing over me right then…

"Dumb, bitch."

Then everything went black.

Twelve Years Earlier

Keisha rode my dick like it was the prize-winning horse in the Kentucky Derby. "Yeah Keisha, ride that dick. Shit, you 'bout to make me cum," I said when her hands pressed down on my thighs and her back faced me. I watched her ass while it moved like waves in the ocean each time she slammed down on me.

Every time she lifted up; I could see her creamy essence as it covered my dick. "This pussy feel good to you, Marcus?" she asked seductively while one of her hands found my nut sack and kneaded it like pizza dough.

I was so far gone in ecstasy that I couldn't answer her, so she asked again, "Nigga, is this pussy good to you or what? I mean, I can get off this muthafucka."

Her frustration and threat to get off my dick broke me from the spell I was under and I finally answered, "Yeah, baby. This shit feels good. This is the best pussy I ever put my dick in. Tell me who this pussy belongs to."

As she came up and tightened her pussy muscles around the head of my dick, she said, "You can own this pussy if you want. It could be yours forever for the right price." As soon as she said it, my shit went limp.

"What the fuck?" she blurted out when my manhood fell out of her.

I pushed her gold-digging ass off of me and asked, "Bitch, why a nigga always got to pay yo ass for that ragged out shit?"

She put her hands on her hips and stated with attitude, "Bitch, who you calling a bitch? And my shit wasn't ragged out a few minutes ago when you was calling my name, muthafucker."

"I'm calling yo ass a bitch. Bitch. Why we can't just fuck without you mentioning money all the damn time and killing the mood?" I stated angrily while I picked my clothes up off the chair.

She looked at me through angry eyes and said, "Nigga, you ain't running up in this shit for free. If you want this pussy for free, then you better make me your girl."

I laughed at what she suggested and said, "My girl? Bitch, you fuck too many niggas around the way for me to claim yo ass." I then peeled off a twenty-dollar bill, threw it at her, and said, "Keep the change, ho. I'm outta here." I didn't even bother tying up my Timbs. I just slid them on in a hurry and left Keisha standing there naked while she cussed my ass out for trying her.

Keisha was just one of the many bitches that had been on my dick ever since I started making paper. When I first met her, I thought I had found someone special. She was thick in all the right places, with hair to the middle of her back. Her hazel eyes and bowlegs made a nigga's eyes roll in the back of my head. At first, I had seriously thought about making her my girl, but then I found out that she made all the niggas eyes roll back. So, I would just go and pick her up when I needed to get my shit off.

I laughed to myself when I reminisced on how these hungry bitches used to turn their heads when I would come through. I would be walking by when they would be all up on the ballers and told myself that one day I'd make those bitches sweat me too. When that day finally arrived, I treated them hoes like the pieces of shit they were.

My cell phone rang as soon as I turned the key in my Expedition. I looked at the caller I.D. and saw that it was Ditto, my connect and the man who gave me the opportunity no one else would. My momma's punk ass boyfriend convinced her to kick me out of the house. He told her I was man enough to take care of myself, and she listened. She wanted a man to love her so bad that her only child was no longer important.

I had nowhere else to go, so I would just roam the streets until I got tired, and then I'd shoot down an abandoned alley and sleep behind the trash dumpsters. Ditto would ride past me every day until one day he finally stopped and asked, "What's up, lil nigga? How come you been sleeping behind the trash bins?"

I gave him a crazy look and did my best to lie, "Man, you ain't seen me sleeping behind no damn dumpsters. That had to be somebody else."

He shook his head, chuckled a little, and then said, "Yeah aiight, if you say so." He then paused as if he had to gather his thoughts and finally said, "I could use a young nigga like you on my team, you feel like putting in some work?"

I had always told myself that I wouldn't push poison out in the streets to my people, so I said to him, "Nah, I'm good."

Ditto shrugged his shoulders and said, "Aiight then, suit yourself."

I began to look at his jewelry and his designer clothes as he pulled a wad of cash out of his pockets. He peeled off ten crisp one-hundred-dollar bills, held them out to me, and said, "Here, go get you a room and something to eat. Oh yeah, and something clean to put on." He paused, wrote something on a piece of paper, and passed it to me and said, "When you're ready, I'll be waiting."

When he started to pull away from the curb, I stopped him and said, “Wait, maybe I could do a little something. But, I don’t wanna do it for long.”

He then unlocked his passenger side door and said, “Get in. I’m about to change your whole world.” That was over a year ago, and I hadn’t slowed down since.

I answered my phone with a slight attitude because my nuts were still full. “What’s up, man?”

“Yo nigga, what’s up with the attitude?” Ditto asked and then laughed at my answer.

“Man, Keisha fuck ass always want a nigga to pay for that community pussy. Bitch should just stand on a corner and pass it out like a wanted poster. What’s going on, my man?”

“Nigga, you shot out, but I need yo ass to stop by when you get a minute,” Ditto said in a more serious tone.

“Damn…everything straight, man? You sound like something wrong,” I said.

“Yeah, nigga. It’s just something I need to put you up on. I’ll be at the trap house on the Southside. Just get here when you can, but don’t take all damn day," Ditto said and then hung up. Click.

I decided to delay the ride to Ditto’s for a minute, so I could stop by and chill with my right hand. Little did I know that the delay would be well worth it.

Chapter Two

I pressed the small baggie into Feelow's hand and asked, "You see that right there?" Feelow looked to where I pointed and saw a thick white girl dip into the alleyway and then finished listening to what he was told, "Go get her for me." Feelow was the only crackhead I trusted around the way. We had come up together, but somehow along life's journey we traveled separate roads. I became the supplier while he became the fiend. However, unlike other crackheads, Feelow could be depended on because he put business before pleasure. Loyalty meant everything to him, and he would rather die than betray his best friend.

Feelow pocketed the baggie and then went on his mission. The girl was thick and fine, with stringy hair that flowed to the middle of her back and looked like it hadn't been brushed in days. Her clothes were wrinkled and looked unwashed, but still through it all her beauty was undeniable. Feelow kept his eyes on the prize as he took off to catch his prey.

***

I would snatch her up by any means necessary because I was going to earn that package in my pocket even if I had to use force. I wondered if she got high too, because I didn't mind sharing what I was just given. I knew there was plenty more where that came from, so I would offer it to her if it came to that. I noticed the girl walk faster, which meant to me that she was trying to get away. I refused to let that happen, so I picked up my pace too. She must not have known that the alley way would end soon, and then she would have nowhere to turn, but straight to me. That is when I would get her.

***

I could hear the footsteps behind me but couldn't force myself to run. The thought of turning my head to see who it was scared the hell out of me. I didn't even know what possessed me to walk through that neighborhood because I had never been on that side of town before. My momma and daddy had probably rolled over in their graves because they had warned me about those same streets. However, those warnings made me even more curious and my curiosity had finally got the best of me.

The footsteps became more rapid, and I knew that soon they would catch up to me. *"Come on feet, don't let me down. Run, Bitch,"* I said to myself, but still they wouldn't take off. All of a sudden, I had noticed that there was nowhere else to go.

"Yeah girl, I got your ass now," the man behind me said as I panicked. I turned to face him but refused to look him in the eyes. I moved from side to side, but everywhere I went he moved right in sync with me.

I pleaded, "Please. Please just let me go, I promise that I'll never come this way again." However, it seemed as if my pleas went unheard.

I pushed my legs to the side and that is when he pounced on me. His arms were wrapped so tight around me that I thought I would quit breathing. "No, let me go, please," I cried out as he pulled me back down the alley in which we'd come. When I felt my feet come up off the ground, I kicked and screamed louder and hoped someone would hear me. "Help me, please! Somebody help me!" However, my cries went unheard as I was steadily being dragged. Then, from out of nowhere, a noise emerged. Click Click.

The man loosened his grip as another man's voice said sternly, "Put her down before you lose both of those arms." I had my eyes closed but the voice made me open them.

"Marcus Man, yo, I was just gonna entertain the little lady and show her a good time." I looked from the man who pointed the gun to the arms of the one who held me and got nervous. I had never seen anyone be killed before and wasn't sure that I was ready to.

The man finally lowered the gun and said to my captor, "Get the fuck outta here before I take your ability to run." The man didn't wait for further instructions, but instead took off back down the alley. I'd felt foolish because I didn't even etch his face into my memory, so if I ever ran into him again, I wouldn't even know it. I told myself that if I made it out of there alive, I would never go that way again.

I looked up at the man who had just rescued me and said two words, "Thank You," and then turned to walk away.

***

Using Feelow to get me bitches had always worked. None of them ever caught on that we were a team. Them hoes thought that I was saving their lives, but to be honest, I didn't give a fuck about them or their lives. Either they fell for the routine or they could get their wigs split. Bitches to me were only good for wetting my dick up and the one I had just saved thought I was just gonna let her walk away. But, that bitch owed me and I needed to be paid.

"Hey, yo Shawty, you just gonna walk off?" I asked, as she stopped in her tracks. She acted like she was afraid to respond, so I walked up on her and said, "Damn, you could at least show a nigga some appreciation." I had never been with a white girl before, but to me, pussy was pussy. I put a hand on her shoulder to try to get her to drop to her knees, but her dirty ass acted like she didn't know what was up. I reached in my pocket to pull out some dope and asked her, "You need a hit or something to get started?"

"No, please don't hit me. I just don't understand what you want," she said in a quick, nervous voice.

"Nah, Ma. I'm talking about a hit of this shit," I said while she looked at me confused, which caused me to ask my next question. "Do you know what this is?"

She shook her head and responded, "No, I've never seen anything like that before." I didn't want to believe her, but something about the look in her eyes told me she was being honest. I put the package back in my pocket and unzipped my pants.

I said to her while I pulled out my dick, "Well, aiight then. But, let a nigga get some of that head." She looked down at my dick as I stroked it, and then the tears formed in her eyes. I wasn't on no rape shit out in the open, so I pushed my dick back in and zipped my pants. I then grabbed her by the arm and said, "You ain't getting out of this shit. Let's go."

No sooner than I got to my ride, my cell rang, "Yo," I answered and felt the girl in front of me jerk. I tightened my grip and said into the phone, "Yeah D, I'm on my way." Dealing with the white girl had made me forget all about Ditto so he had a slight attitude.

When I answered his call he snapped, "Yo, nigga, where the fuck you at? Ain't shit out there more important than business, especially when you dealing with me."

I said, "Yo man, my bad, something came up on the way, but I'm headed there now."

He responded, "Muthafucka, you got ten minutes." Click.

When the call ended, I put my phone back in my pocket and opened the passenger door. "Get your ass in there. You riding with me till I get what the fuck I want," I said, and at that moment, the little bitch became bold.

"How you gonna save me from another man and then treat me like shit?" She crossed her arms over her chest and continued, "You should have just let the motherfucker take me." For some reason her attitude turned me on and caused me to soften up.

"Yo. Just chill, Ma. I'ma get you cleaned up and see what you about. But, right now, I got business to handle," I said to her as I drove away.

***

I pulled up to the stash house and thought about my next move. I didn't know the bitch beside me, so I wasn't sure about taking her in with me, but I also didn't want to leave her outside. I was too afraid that she would try to run. I turned to her and said, "Get out." Something about the way she looked at me sent chills down my spine, but I shook that shit off and got out. She still sat in the ride so I went around to the passenger side and yanked the door open and said "Yo, you act like your ass can't hear or something. Let's fucking go."

She turned her body towards me and when she looked in my eyes, it felt like I could see inside of her. I felt like I could feel her pain, and it pissed me off because it also made me feel mine. It reminded me of the days before Ditto came along. The days when no one gave a fuck about me, and it almost made me wanna comfort her. Almost. "Man, get the fuck out," I said angrily as I grabbed her by the wrist and pulled her out of the seat. She stumbled when her feet hit the ground but caught herself. I shut the door and turned to her and said, "When we go in here don't say shit to anybody. Do you understand?" She nodded yes and then followed behind me as I walked up the porch steps.

I opened the door and found a pistol pointed at me and asked, "Yo, what the fuck?" The man behind the pistol was Ditto's top lieutenant named Stone, and I knew if I made one wrong move, I'd lose my head. Stone was a killer and if Ditto said shoot, it didn't matter who was on the other end of the gun. Stone had killed his own brother at Ditto's demand because he tried to betray him. Stone had overheard him on the phone saying he was going to get information about Ditto to help the feds set him up. When Stone told Ditto, they began to dig deeper and found out more than they bargained for, so Ditto ordered the execution and the rest was history.

I heard Ditto's voice as he emerged from behind his boy. He asked, "Who the fuck gave you permission to bring company up in here?" When I first got under Ditto, he treated me like a son, but as soon as my status grew, he became resentful and often treated me like the enemy. I swore that one day I would break free from his grasp, but I knew I would have to put him six feet deep first.

I knew I should have left the bitch in the car, but I didn't want to risk it. At least not before I got the pussy. I opened my mouth to answer him, but a voice from behind me beat me to it." Krystal.

My name is Krystal, and he just saved my life. I'm not a trick." Ditto walked from behind his boy and stood face to face with me. We stared at each other for a minute and then he motioned for me to step to the side. I was hesitant at first, but the bitch wasn't worth a bullet so I moved.

***

He was so close to me I could feel his breath on my skin. When my heart sped up, I closed my eyes and said a silent prayer. The man that stood in front of me smirked and then said, "You got some balls white girl and although, I find that shit sexy, your dirty ass wasn't asked to speak." He paused and lifted his hand to my hair and as he brushed his fingers through it, he said "Yo Stone, clean this bitch up."

I looked to the man who had saved my life and panicked hoping he would save me again. "Yo Ditto, I got that so chill with that shit. What am I here for?" he asked.

Ditto turned to face him and said, "One of your lil niggas need to be dealt with."

Ditto finally moved away from me and I breathed a sigh of relief. Marcus looked at him confused and asked, "What the fuck you talking about, D?"

Ditto responded in a low tone,"Ya boy Milo been cutting off the product. Seems like the lil nigga got a problem."

Marcus cut him off and said, "Nah nigga, that shit can't be true. I would have noticed." Ditto pulled out his cell phone and an image of who I presumed to be Milo showed up on the screen. Marcus watched as he pulled a package out of his pocket. He looked around nervously to make sure no one was watching him and then he broke a piece off. He then pulled a glass pipe out from under the cushion and filled it with a hard substance. Marcus' eyes widened as the man put the pipe to his lips and lit it. He looked as if he were deep in pleasure as the smoke filled his lungs. The sweat formed on his forehead and then he suddenly jumped up and stashed the pipe back where he got it from right before another worker walked in.

Ditto said, "I got several calls from the street generals saying we got some unhappy customers. Niggas trying to get they dick sucked, but them hoes ain't taking crumbs. Don't nobody fuck with my shit or my money like that. I don't even allow my own momma to be a dollar short." Ditto's mom Delores was a fiend and one of his best customers.

Marcus nodded his head and asked, “How you want me to handle it?”

Ditto responded in a stern voice, “Eliminate that muthafucka.” Marcus didn’t say another word, but instead grabbed my arm.

As we proceeded to leave, Ditto spoke up, “Nah nigga, leave your piece here.”

Marcus looked confused and raised an eyebrow, then asked, “How the fuck you expect me to handle this nigga without my piece?”

Ditto laughed at his question and stated, “Nah, not that piece.” Then he pointed to me. “That one.”

Chapter Three

I felt uneasy when I left the white girl with Ditto and Stone. Ditto once had a wife who burned him by sleeping with a federal agent who tried to set him up along with Stone's brother. She tried to deny it, but when she came up pregnant, he knew she was lying. She swore it was his, but Ditto was sterile from a childhood bike accident. He knew that he could cum in a bitch all day with no repercussions, but his wife never had a clue. Rumor was he paid a fiend to run up in their house while they were sleeping and rob them at gunpoint. Ditto was shot twice, once in the arm and once in the shoulder. His wife was shot through the heart. A week later, that same fiend was found floating face down in the river. Ditto played the heartbroken husband for a while, but ever since then he held no respect for a woman, not even his own momma.

I pulled up to Milo's baby momma's house and knocked on the door. It took a few minutes, but Netta finally answered. Netta had been on my dick for a minute and every chance she got, she tested the waters. "Mmm, I hope you here to lay some pipe because your boy damn sure ain't," she said as she looked at me seductively. Her nipples were hard and poked through the t-shirt she had on.

My dick hadn't been sucked since Keisha's fuck ass tried me, so I finally decided to take her up on her offer. "Where ya nigga at?" I asked, and then licked my lips.

She smiled and answered, "Hell if I know. His black ass ain't been by in three days. Nigga ain't even dropped off no damn diaper money for his son." I knew then that she didn't know about his new-found habit and I wasn't gonna leave her with that as a last impression.

I stepped in further as she closed the door behind me and then dropped to her knees. I released the beast from my boxers while I looked down at her and said, "Damn Netta, yo ass ain't playing."

She looked up at me as she gripped my dick in her hand and said, "Nigga, I been wanting to swallow this dick, but you selfish with it. Now I'm gonna take advantage of it." Then she pulled it between her lips. Netta sucked my dick slow and hard, but I had shit to handle so I needed to hurry up.

I pulled back from her and said, "Go bend that ass over. I'm about to tear that pussy up." She smiled and hopped up and then walked over to the couch. When she got there, she bent over the back of it, spread her ass cheeks, and said, "Come on, Marcus. This shit already wet just thinking about it."

I could see her pussy juice as it glistened in the light and when I put my dick to her hole, Milo walked in. He stood in shock for a second and then stormed over to where we were. "Nigga, the fuck you doing with my bitch?" he asked. My dick shriveled up instantly as Milo looked from me to her.

I put it back in my pants and zipped up and said to him, "I wouldn't need to be with your bitch if your ass was home sucking on the pussy instead of that glass dick."

Netta gasped and looked at Milo with an angry face and asked, "What the fuck is he talking about, Milo?"

Milo shook his head, sniffed as if he had just snorted a line, and responded in an agitated voice, "Bitch, I know you don't believe that shit, and anyway take yo ass in the room with my son."

The look Milo gave her made her do as he said and when she left, I said to him, "Let's take a ride."

He hesitated and started to speak, but I pulled my nine from under the back of my shirt and stopped him. "You had something to say, lil nigga?" I asked, and then pointed to the door.

When we got to the ride and got in, Milo started to sing like a bird, "Yo man I slipped up, but it won't happen again." I pulled out of the driveway and headed to the warehouse.

I didn't speak a word the whole ride there, but as soon as we pulled in I spoke, "You been fucking up the product and my boy ain't happy. What the fuck happened, nigga?"

He shook his head and told me the story, "Man, I was tricking with that bitch Terry, and she talked me into it and then one thing led to another. I tried to control it, but that shit was calling me. Man, I fucked up. My dick don't even get hard no more."

I looked at him and told myself that killing him would be the right thing to do, I said, "Get outta the ride."

He then pleaded for his life. "Marcus, come on man. I slipped up. I won't do it again, man. I swear." I looked in his eyes and knew that he was lying because once you made that wrong turn, you ran into dead ends and there would be no turning back. He pled one more time for his life, "Come on, dawg," and then, I pulled the trigger. I called the cleaning crew before I left the warehouse, and then I called Ditto.

He answered on the first ring, "What it do, my man?"

I said one word back to him, "Done." Then I hung up.

***

When Marcus walked out and left me with his boys, I didn't know what was going to happen. The one named Ditto looked at me and shook his head before he dialed a number. He continued his stare as he spoke into the phone, "Get your ass over here and make sure you don't have no panties on." His stare didn't waver even after he hung up. His boy Stone stood against the wall with his hand on the pistol that was tucked into his waistline.

I looked from one to the other and then held my head down. Nobody said a word as the minutes passed, which caused an uncomfortable aura. Finally, a knock sounded at the door. Ditto nodded his head at Stone, who then went to answer the door.

***

I wasn't happy about having Milo's blood on my hands, but it came with the job. He wasn't the first I'd killed, and I knew that he wouldn't be the last. When I first came on board with Ditto, he told me I had to prove my loyalty and show him I could be trusted. My first kill was an old man who had shorted Ditto on his money. I wondered who would mourn his death as I pushed a slug between his eyes and then walked away with no remorse. After that, killing came easy to me and nobody was off limits. I headed back to Dittos, so I could scoop up the white bitch, but when I got there, I wasn't prepared for what I saw.

***

Stone walked back into the living room with a female carrying a duffel bag. She was tall and skinny like a model and walked right up to Ditto. She put her hands on her hips, cocked her head to the side, and said, "Nigga, you ain't tell me it was a white bitch."

Ditto reached a hand up and pulled her closer by the edges of her short skirt and said, "Bitch, it don't matter what fucking color she is. Handle your fucking business." He then nodded his head forward and the girl dropped to her knees in front of him. She unzipped his jeans and as he looked over into my eyes he said, "And you better wet up every inch of this muthafucka." I was still a virgin and wondered if all dicks were that big. I had heard the saying about black men before and seeing Dittos dick made it true. I remembered when Marcus pulled his out earlier in the alley and tried to compare the two, but they were about the same. I turned my head away while the girls head bobbed up and down. Slurping sounds filled the room and I tried my hardest not to steal peeks. Stone remained standing against the wall as if their acts didn't affect him and then all movement stopped.

The girl got up from her knees and turned towards me. Her back faced Ditto as he stood up from the chair he sat in. She gave me a dirty look as Ditto bent her over the table in front of her. Once again, he and I made contact as he spread her open and entered her. I wanted to jump up and run, but from the look on Stone's face I knew that I wouldn't make it very far so, I just sat there and listened as the sounds of sex filled the air. "Yeah, Ditto. Oh, shit. This dick is good. Damn!" the girl cried out as he slid in and out of her.

She looked up at me and said, "Bitch, I'm gonna make you so damn pretty after I get this dick. Ooh, yes. Shit!"

My heart sped up as Ditto spoke, "You ever had dick like this before? Huh, white girl?" His words came out broken because of his rhythm. I wasn't sure if I was supposed to answer him, so I didn't and my silence made him speak again. "A nigga got to clean yo dirty ass up. Yeah, shit. I bet you real pretty under all that dirt. Ah, shit." He closed his eyes and slammed into the girl harder.

Their bodies collided and made a clapping sound. "Yeah Ditto, make this pussy cum. Yes. Oh, yes. I'm cumming." He then pulled out of her and she turned back around to face him. When she did, she pulled his dick back into her mouth.

Ditto said to me, "Marcus ain't gonna give you dick like this. Shit. Ah, fuck. I'm cumming. Catch that shit."

When he fell out of her mouth, his dick fell limp against his thigh. Ditto then pulled his pants back up but didn't bother to zip them. Instead, he sat back down in the chair and waved his hand at the girl while his eyes stared into mine. The girl pushed her short skirt back up and picked up her duffle bag. She walked over to me, shook her head, and said, "Nigga, you paying me extra for this one."

***

I pulled up to the trap house and nervously turned off the engine of my ride. I was afraid of what I'd find when I walked in. I knew Ditto all too well and because of his lack of respect for women, I was worried that he'd already done something to the white girl. My mind went to the last girl I'd had around Ditto. He needed me to drop off a package out of town and instead of waiting for me to come get it, he came to the motel where I had the girl. The girl was still naked when he walked in, and because of that, he knew the bitch didn't mean shit to me. After we discussed our business, he pulled his dick out and made her suck it until her jaws got sore. I couldn't do shit, but sit there and listen as he moaned while she slobbed all over him.

When he came in her mouth, she gagged, but he held her head down with his hand and made her swallow every drop. I thought he would make the bitch choke to death as he sat there and laughed. All I could do was shake my head. He finally asked me, "Are you gonna sit there and watch my dick, or you gonna deliver my shit?" I didn't say a word. I got up from the chair, walked out the room, and left him and the bitch to do whatever. I never saw the girl again after that.

I hoped that he hadn't done the same thing to the white girl. For some reason, I felt real protective over her. I knocked on the door this time because it was locked, and then Stone opened it. He laughed. "Nigga, what the fuck is so damn funny?" I asked and expected a bullshit answer but got nothing. Stone stepped aside, so I could walk all the way in and when I did, I didn't see the girl anywhere. I looked at Ditto as he sat in his chair with his pants undone while he chewed on a straw.

He asked with raised eyebrows, "Did you handle that?" I wondered why he asked me that after I had already called and told him.

"I did." I asked him in a confused manner, "Man, I already hit you up and told you I did. Why you questioning me now?"

Ditto stood up and walked all the way up on me. While he looked me in my eyes he said, "I wanted to hear you say it again while you look me in the face."

I immediately went off. "Damn D, I been with you all this time and you all of a sudden questioning me. What's up with that?"

He walked back to his chair and sat down before he answered, "That's because you slipped, my nigga. You should have caught that shit without me telling you. Then you bring a white bitch up in this muthafucka without permission."

I cut him off before he said another word. "Yo, that white bitch didn't mean shit. I was just trying to get my shit off and then she was gonna be..." A sudden movement stopped my words. I turned my head, looked to where the movement came from, and saw the most beautiful woman I had ever seen.

"My name ain't white bitch. It's Krystal."

***

The look in Marcus' eyes when I walked in was not one that I expected. The girl had cleaned me up, and I looked like my old self again. I knew it was a surprise to him from the look on his face. Somehow, Ditto saw under all the disarray and found the me I was before all the heartache and loss. I stared at Marcus with attitude as he walked closer to me. When he was right in front of me, Ditto laughed and said, "You lucky I saw something in her, or she would be sucking my dick right now."

***

"Damn." That was all I could manage to say as I looked Krystal in her big green eyes.

She looked back at me with a painful glare and said, "I don't have nowhere to go. So please don't put me back out there."

My chest pounded from the adrenaline rush I was feeling. I had misjudged her for trash like the other girls I'd picked up, but instead, I'd found a diamond in the rough and wondered what else I may find.

I said to her without breaking my stare, "Damn, you're beautiful, Ma. Don't worry, I'ma keep you around for a minute. Just don't make me regret around for a minute."

***

When Marcus and I left the trap house, we left ten kilos heavier. I didn't know anything about drugs because I had never been around them. Marcus could tell that I was nervous, so he gently took my hand in his and said, "Ain't nothing gonna happen to you while you with me, so stop looking like that. Trust me, I got you." He squeezed my hand tighter and continued, "I'm gonna always have you." And I believed him.

Chapter Four

The pressure around my heart was as tight as the cuffs around my wrists. Everyone watched as I walked out of the courthouse to an awaiting police car where a female deputy stood with the back door open.

"Dumb bitch."

Marcus' words played over and over in my mind as my pulse sped up. I ducked my head, so I could get in the back seat and when the door closed behind me, I looked up.

I locked eyes with Marcus and mouthed the words I Love You to him. I continued my stare as the car pulled out of the parking spot. I took one last look at Marcus as he put his arm around another female and kissed her on the cheek. Her stomach poked out a little and revealed a small baby bump. I felt the tears form in my eyes. Marcus laughed.

The ride to the jail was long and quiet. My young mind tried to process what I had just seen. Maybe I took things out of context, but I know what I saw. Could I have been that naïve?

I thought about the baby Marcus and I had created. I thought he would have been so happy when I told him, but I was wrong. He said we didn't need to bring a baby into this world as long as we were living the fast life. I begged him, but my cries went unheard.

The day he took me to get an abortion was the saddest day of my life, but he gave me no other option. It was either him or the life that grew inside of me. How do you choose between two people you love? I had no one, but him and couldn't image my life without him in it, so I let the doctor suck my baby right out of me.

"Dumb Bitch.

Chapter Five

Marcus pulled up in front of a two-story condominium and got out without saying a word to me. I jumped when he slammed his door shut and was afraid to move. I only sat for a minute before my door was yanked open. "Yo, you pretty as fuck, but you act like you slow or something," he said to me as he looked in my eyes. We stared each other down for a second and then he shook his head and said, "Get the fuck out and grab that duffle bag outta the back." He then turned around and walked away.

I jumped out of his ride and opened the back door to retrieve the bag. I didn't know how much ten kilos of cocaine was supposed to weigh, but the bag was heavy when I slung it over my shoulder.

"Ugh," I grunted as I closed the door behind me and turned to follow Marcus. He was at the front door of his condo and waited for me as I lugged the bag to him. When I got to the door, I dropped it on the ground and said, "It's good to know I'm dealing with a piece of shit." Then I walked in and left him and the bag outside.

***

The ride to my condo seemed longer than usual because of the silence between me and Krystal. I cut my eyes at her because I just couldn't help myself. I had never taken a female to the place I rested my head, but something inside of me told me that was where she belonged. I figured if I treated her like shit she wouldn't be able to get inside my head. I hadn't even smelled the pussy yet, but somehow I felt hooked. I didn't know if it was her beauty, her obvious innocence, or her boldness that drew me in, but she had already made me slip once by taking her to the trap house. I had to be careful with her or I could very well slip again.

***

I'd never had a boyfriend before, and I wasn't sure what Marcus would end up being to me. I didn't know what purpose I served by him taking me with him, although, I didn't care because I had nowhere else to go. I would do whatever I had to do as long as he let me stay.

When I entered his condo, I was mesmerized by the beauty of it. I could tell he had his shit together and was doing good for himself. I had always been attracted to black men, especially those with thugged out personalities like Marcus. It was something about his swag that brought me chills. The thought of his smooth dark flesh against my pale skin was a beautiful combination. That dope boy attitude full of power was enough to take my breath away. As I stood there deep in thought, Marcus walked up behind me, dropped the bag at my feet, and said, "You putting in work if you stay up in my shit, and nobody is welcome in this bitch. If I find out you brought somebody here, I won't hesitate to split your wig. You hear me?"

I looked at him through evil eyes and stated with attitude, "Is that how you're going to treat me all the time because if it is, you can take my white ass back where you got me from."

He laughed and shook his head and said, "Yeah. You wasn't fairing too well then, and you keep talking shit you won't be fairing too well now either." He paused and looked me deep in the eyes, and then said, "Pick that shit up and follow me." I wanted to be stubborn and not do what he said, but my options were few so I bent my ass over and picked up the bag.

I followed him and watched as he placed his thumb over the eye of a portrait on the wall. When he did, the wall slipped up and opened, revealing a staircase leading down. He was smart, because there was no way anyone could have noticed it without prior knowledge. It was a little too trusting of me, so I knew that if I betrayed him, I would pay for it dearly. He looked back at me before he descended the staircase and snatched the bag out of my hand. I continued to follow and as soon as my foot touched the second stair, the wall closed.

***

I didn't know why I felt like I could trust the white girl. I had never trusted another woman after my momma did me dirty, but something inside of me told me that she was a rider. I was hard with her because I needed to make sure she could stand in the mud even if it turned to quicksand, and I wasn't beyond killing her if I found weaknesses behind her tough exterior.

I led her down the stairs and when I threw the duffel bag on the table, she flinched. "It's a little too late to be jumpy, so if you ain't gonna be able to handle this, tell me now," I said to her with a serious look on my face.

She took a second and then lit in on my ass. "Tell you now, so you can what? So you can put a bullet between my fucking eyes? Huh, Marcus? I'm not a veteran in the streets, but I'm not a dumb ass white girl either." Tears formed in her big green eyes as she continued. "Yeah, I can handle whatever you throw at me. You kno why, Marcus? Because I don't have a choice. I'm all done in this world and, although, you're a piece of shit you're all I fucking got."

My heart sped up as her tears flowed, but I refused to comfort her. Instead, I pushed a kilo across the table to her and said, "Dry that shit up. I'm about to make you a boss bitch."

***

I walked over to the table and placed a hand on the cocaine but was unsure of what to do next so I just stood there and waited for further instructions. Marcus cut his eyes up at me and said, "Open that drawer under the table and pull out those beakers and bottles of come back." He paused as I did what he told me and then said, "Oh yeah, make sure you pull out a knife and scale too."

I knew what beakers were from my high school chemistry class, but for some reason they felt foreign to me. I saw tiny bottles of white powder labeled **COME BACK,** pulled them out along with the beakers, and said, "Okay, I think I'm ready now."

I watched as he pulled out two boxes of baking soda and two small hot plates, and then he said, "Oh, yeah. Well, I hope you ready for this dick later on too."

I didn't respond at first because I didn't know what to say. I had never been with a man before, but I was too afraid to tell him so I talked shit back instead, "Yeah, usually men who talk about their dicks have small ones."

He laughed and said, "Aiight, white girl. I'm gonna shut up until it's time to put in that work, and then you can tell me just how small my dick is." Then he went back to the task at hand.

Chapter Six

My cell buzzed as soon as I put the lighter to the pipe. "Fuck!" I said out loud with a frustrated voice. It was time for my first hit of the day, and I had put a boulder on the glass dick I had between my lips. However, I tried to make sure I always answered my phone, so I didn't lose focus on the important things in my life. I put the pipe down on the bed beside me and picked the phone up. "What it do?" I asked, while I stared at the pipe and licked my lips. Everyone knew that the first hit of the day was the best one, and I wanted that shit as bad as a dick wanted pussy. I got chill bumps once I heard the voice on the other end. "Yo Fee, what's up lil nigga? I need you to come see me. I got a job for you," Ditto said into the phone. I didn't fuck with him like that, so I wondered what was up.

I had met Ditto through Marcus and had only been around him a few times, so for him to call me instead of Marcus told me that he had some malice on his mind. I asked, "Why you calling me instead of your boy? I don't work for you."

He responded, "Well, since Marcus works for me, and you work for him, then that means you handle my shit. So like I said, I need to see you." He paused for a second and continued, "So you comin or should I come get you?" I'd been able to hide my addiction well and as far as I knew no one, but Marcus was aware of it, and that's how I wanted to keep it.

Marcus and I grew up in the same projects together and when his momma had one of her boyfriends over, he would stay with me, so he wouldn't have to hear her get her guts tore up all night. However, my pops was given a job in another city and forced us to move away. So, when Marcus got kicked out of his mom's place, he had nowhere to go. I had heard he was living in the streets until Ditto swiped him up and put him on.

When I had to move away from my best friend, it was like losing a brother, but I soon found another friend and her pussy had me strung out. One day, she introduced me to crack, and the rest was history. I thought I was in love and then one day I walked in and saw another nigga's dick inside of her. My heart had completely broke, so I went home and packed a bag and went back to the only person I knew had my back no matter what. When I told Marcus about my habit, he said, "Nigga, you still my boy. I got you as long as you keep that shit under control." So far, I'd been able to keep my habit at bay. No matter how loud it called my name, I vowed I'd never fuck up Marcus' shit and because of his faith and trust in me, I'd rather die than let him down.

"I got a couple of moves to make, but I'll be there," I said to Ditto as my heart sped up.

Then he said back to me, "Nah nigga, make this your first move." Click. After he hung up, I threw my phone on the bed and looked down at my pipe. I knew as bad as I wanted that wake up, it would have to wait because I was sure Ditto would be able to notice it. Business was always before pleasure with me, so I got my black ass up and prepared myself to face him.

I told myself that I should call Marcus first because something told me that he had no idea about the call I had just received. However, I went against my better judgement and decided I'd tell him about it later. I wanted to find out what was up with Ditto's grimy ass first. I hopped in my ride and turned the key and as soon as I backed out of my parking spot to meet up with Ditto, my phone buzzed again.

***

Feelow didn't know that I knew about his habit, but I could pick up on the signs no matter how deep he hid it. I had also been put on the information but wanted to wait until the right time to use it. My momma was a crackhead, so I knew one when I saw one. I had only encountered Feelow a few times when he would be with Marcus, and I swore that I could see it in his eyes. "Yo Stone, let's go. I wanna pick up Crackhead Carla on the way, so I can give this lil nigga something to do while I taunt his ass." Crackhead Carla use to cum for me because all a nigga had to do was look at her fine ass and the pre cum would push its way to the top. However, she let one of her girls talk her into taking a hit and that hit turned into a habit and the rest was history. I was going to use the pussy and the crack to try to pull Freelow from Marcus.

When I first ran across Marcus, he was an eighteen-year-old homeless kid. I picked that little nigga up and took him under my wing. My intention was to make him my heir to the game, but the more money he made, the more arrogant and unappreciative he got. It was time I cut his ass back down to size so he would realize that I was still the muthafuckin boss.

***

I searched my mind on the way to meet Ditto, thinking of what he possibly could have wanted because I knew it couldn't have been good. I really didn't want to leave without that hit, but I needed a clear head to deal with that nigga. My gut told me that some shit was being cooked up and if it was anything to betray Marcus, Ditto could kiss my black ass. I'd rather eat a muthafuckin bullet than stab my nigga in the back.

***

Feelow never ignored my calls, so I got instantly worried. I hoped that his ass hadn't fucked around and overdosed on that shit. I imagined my nigga spread out somewhere with his heart about to bust out of his chest, and it fucked up my whole line of concentration. I decided to try him one more time before I went to check on him.

***

I'm not sure why I was nervous about answering the phone when I saw that it was Marcus. I always answered his calls and knew that if I didn't answer this one, he would feel some type of way. "Yo my nigga, what's good?" I asked with a slight nervousness in my voice.

"Damn man, a nigga was getting worried. I thought you done fucked around and put a mountain on that hilltop. You good?" Marcus said as I listened and then answered.

"Nah man, I had my shit on vibrate and had my tunes bumping. I just happened to look over and saw the light blinking on my phone. What's up?"

Marcus responded, "Aye, I need you to pull through the bottom and pick up that sneaker money for me. Can you handle that?"

"Yeah man, but I'm about to go see this fine redbone I met up at the store the other day. Just let me catch this nut and I'll go handle that for you." The lie came out of my lips too easy and I regretted it, but it was too late to change it.

I could hear the doubt in Marcus' voice when he spoke back to me, "Aiight, man. Push a stroke up in that bitch for me. Holla at me when you pull through." Then the call disconnected.

I don't know why I chose to lie to Marcus because it was something I'd never done before. I just always felt like I didn't need to. I instantly became paranoid because my mind told me that he could sense it. However, I pushed that thought out of my head and continued on to my destination.

***

I felt the lie before it even left his lips. Feelow had never lied to me before, even if he knew the truth would piss me off. I threw the beaker against the wall and felt my heart quicken. "Fuck!" I said out loud as the glass shattered.

It startled Krystal and she asked in a frightened voice, "What's wrong? What did I do?"

I leaned against the wall, slid down to the floor without answering her, and cradled my head in my hands. She walked over and kneeled beside me as my mind turned flips. I felt her hand when she laid it over mine and looked up. There was no way she could understand what I was feeling. Feelow was like a brother to me, and he had never betrayed me, but I could tell by the sound of his voice that he was planning to. Disloyalty meant death in the drug world and killing him would be like pulling the trigger on myself and committing suicide. The question was, if it came to that, could I do it?

I looked up into Krystal's eyes and pulled her into me for a kiss, but she pulled back and said something that fucked me up even more, "Marcus, I've never been with a man, so I need you to be patient with me." I was shocked at the revelation and let her go. I pushed her away from me because I would be in beast mode until I found out what was going on with my boy, which meant I needed to take my frustration out on a lesser bitch.

I got up from where I sat and told Krystal, "Keep doing what I taught you. I gotta make a run. I'm trusting you with my shit, so don't make me regret it."

***

I didn't know what was going on with Marcus, but after he made that phone call, his attitude totally changed. It hurt my feelings when he pushed me away as I tried to comfort him. I had only met him that morning, but I felt I knew he was about to go fuck something up and there was nothing I could have done to stop him.

***

I knew I was off balance when I left the white girl to handle my shit, but Feelow made me feel some type of way. I wouldn't know for certain until I looked him in his eyes. I had hoped my mind was playing tricks on me. I didn't feel like Krystal would do anything stupid while I was gone. Somehow, I felt that she was smarter than your average chick, but if I was wrong about it, I wouldn't hesitate to kill the bitch. Right then, I needed to fuck something up and a warm wet pussy was the answer.

Chapter Seven

I pulled up to the spot where Ditto told me to meet him and got even more nervous. My hand slightly shook when I went to knock on the door. Ditto's right-hand man, Stone opened it up and nodded his head for me to step inside, but before I did, he patted me down. I looked at him and said, "Yo man, I know better."

He was a man of few words, but managed to say to me, "Protocol. You gotta problem with it?"

I said confidently, "Nah, we good." I proceeded to walk inside.

I could smell it before I even made it all the way inside. The aroma slowed down my pace and sped up my adrenaline. When I made it to the living room, I found the source. Crackhead Carla was standing up butt ass naked in front of Ditto with her legs spread wide. He sat in the chair and looked up at her while he rubbed a finger over her enlarged clit as she inhaled the clouds of smoke that came from the glass pipe. When she exhaled and stepped back, it caused Ditto to look up and straight at me. He laughed and stood up and then told Carla, "Sit yo ass in that chair and spread them legs, so I can see that pussy." She hesitated at first, but when Ditto looked at her crazy she obliged.

He walked over to me and asked, "Yo Fee, which one you want more? That fat ass pussy over there?" He pulled a package of rocks out of his pocket and continued, "Or these fat ass rocks?"

I squinted my eyes in confusion and said, "Nah, D. You tripping, man. I don't fuck around like that. I just came here to see what's up."

He turned away from me and walked back over to where Carla sat. He stood to the back of the chair, so he would be behind her and pulled his dick and balls out and said, "Lean your head back and suck on these balls while I handle this business."

She leaned her head back as far as it would go and pulled Ditto's sagging nuts into her mouth as he put a hand around his dick and stroked it. I turned my head away and said in an agitated voice, "Nigga, what the fuck you call me over here for? I got shit to do."

He summoned me over to him and Carla, and then told her to stop what she was doing. He pulled his dick and balls back and reached into his pocket to retrieve what held her there. He looked into my eyes while he spoke to her, “This is for him. Pull out his dick and suck it for him while he enjoys it. Make him feel as good as you did me.”

I swallowed hard as a lump formed in my throat and said, “Nah, D. I told you I don’t fuck around like that, so why you fucking with me?” He didn’t respond and the quietness of the room made the sizzle of the dope sound louder. I looked down at Carla as she melted the big boulder on the pipe and as the sweat formed on my forehead, she passed it my way.

***

I could see it in his eyes while the dope melted. The sound of his desire caused beads of sweat to form on his brow. I figured it may take a minute, but he would have no choice, but to give it. He looked from me to the pipe and weighed his options. How I treated him from that moment on would be based on the choices he made.

***

I licked my lips as I looked down at the pipe. I had already missed my wakeup call because of Ditto and if I didn’t know anything else, I knew that if I reached for that pipe, I would be doomed from that point on. My heart sped up, and my dick got hard just from the thought of it filling my lungs. I looked up into Ditto’s eyes and then reached for the pipe.

***

I knocked on Tracy’s door like I was the police about to do a bust. It took her a minute to come to the door and when she did, she was dressed in nothing, but a thong and tank top. I had met Tracy at the strip club and the way she grinded her ass on the pole had my nuts about to burst. I ended up giving her all the ends I had in my pocket and a promise to stop by her crib. However, other things kept standing in my way of stopping by, but that night I was gonna take out my frustrations on her and blow her back out. She smiled when she saw it was me and said, "Damn. What blew your sexy ass in my direction?"

I walked in without answering and immediately began to take off my clothes. When I was down to only my boxers, I finally spoke, "A nigga needs a pole dance, and I couldn't think of anyone better to do it."

She smacked her lips and replied, "Oh, so you think you gonna stand me up one second and then walk in here another second, and I'm just supposed to bow down and handle you? Nigga, you got some nerve."

I pulled my dick out of the slit in my boxers and stroked it as I said, "Come on over here and take that attitude out on this dick right here."

She smiled as she walked closer and said, "Damn nigga, it's gonna take two pussies to handle all that meat."

As soon as she said it, a thick redbone walked into the living room and said, "Don't worry, Trace. I got your back."

***

After I finished cooking the dope for Marcus, I left the underground room and went upstairs to explore the rest of his place. I found the kitchen first because a bitch was hungry. There wasn't much in the fridge, but I managed to nibble enough to satisfy my hunger. I instantly became jealous as thoughts of him going to another woman entered my mental. That phone call had really upset him and because I didn't know him that well, I wasn't sure what he was capable of.

I cleaned up my mess and went upstairs to hopefully find a shower. I was exhausted, and I knew the water would help me relax. His bathroom was immaculate, decorated in all white. I looked in the cabinets to check for signs of another woman but found none. I smiled at the thought of my stuff lining those very shelves.

After I soaked in the hot water until it turned cold, I got out and wrapped a towel around me. I then went into his bedroom and found a t-shirt to put on, and the size of it swallowed my short statue. I didn't know when Marcus would return, nor did I know how to contact him, so I laid down on his bed and instantly drifted off to sleep.

***

"Yeah, shit. Come on and sit that fat pussy on this muthafucka," I said in a sex filled voice while Tracy and the redbone slobbed on my dick and balls. When they came up the redbone tried to get me to eat her pussy, but I didn't know where that bitch had been, so that shit wasn't happening. So instead, I made Tracy get on all four and as I tore her walls down, she feasted on the redbone.

***

After I got my shit off, I decided to go check on the mission that Feelow was supposed to handle. When I pulled up at the bottom, one of my workers greeted me. "Yo what's up, Marcus. We been waiting on you to come through," Trap said as he motioned the other worker named Creep over.

I got out my ride and asked, "Hey, has Feelow pulled through here yet?"

Trap answered while he shook his head, "Nah, Boss Man. We ain't seen that nigga."

Creep saw the look on my face and asked, "Is everything alright?"

"I don't know, but I asked him to stop by hours ago and he claimed he had to make another stop first," I said with even more concern in my voice. Trap and Creep looked at each other and then back to me.

Creep said, "Dawg, I ain't implying anything, but shit don't sound right."

Then Trap cut in, “Fee ain’t never missed a pickup. Business always comes first for him. I hope that nigga alright.” To my knowledge, I was the only one who knew about Feelow’s habit and did what I could to keep it that way. I decided to try his cell again and see if I could find out what was up.

When he didn’t answer, I looked at Trap and Creep and said, “If he does show up here, call me immediately and don’t let him leave until I get here.” I then grabbed the book bag from Creep and took my black ass home.

During the ride back home, I thought about Feelow and wondered what the fuck could be going on. I hoped that he was okay because the thought of something happening to my boy had me on edge. I would kill anybody who had the balls to fuck with him. Jesus himself could get it when it came to Feelow.

I pulled up in front of my condo and noticed all the lights were off. I figured the white girl must have gotten tired of waiting on my ass and called it a night. However, I pulled my piece out just in case I was wrong. I walked in slowly and then checked everywhere downstairs. When I went down to my hidden room, I noticed that she had finished the task I had given her. There were thirty cookies on the plastic sheet. They were thick and perfectly formed with a light tan color. I was actually impressed at the sight before me and was pleased when I weighed the product. Everything was on point, as if I performed the job myself.

After looking around downstairs, I went up to the second floor and did the same check. I finally walked into my bedroom, which is when I noticed her. The moonlight shined on her through the window and made her look like an angel sent from heaven. She was beautiful, and I couldn’t help but stand there and stare at her for a minute and then went to wash off the pussy from my earlier escapade. After my shower, I dried off and walked back to the bed with my dick swinging. When I climbed in bed beside her, she woke up.

“Hey, I’m glad you made it back okay. I hope everything’s okay,” she said and I could feel her concern in her words but didn’t understand it. She didn’t even know me, so I wondered why she cared.

I answered her in a soft voice, “I’m good. Just worried about a friend of mine. Some shit don’t feel right.” I looked over into her eyes and finished, “I had to leave. I didn’t want to take that shit out on you.”

She sat up in the bed and removed the t-shirt she had on. Her small nipples stood erect on her porcelain white breasts. She lied back down, looked over at me, and said, “Teach me how to please you, Marcus. I don’t ever want you to have to find comfort in some-one else.”

Chapter Eight

I grabbed the pipe from Carla and threw it across the room. She jumped at the shattering sound and then proceeded to cuss my ass out, "You motherfucker. That was my best pipe. Nigga, you gonna pay for that shit." She got up and ran over to where the pipe had fallen and looked for the brillo that she had just melted the big boulder on.

I looked at Ditto and through angry eyes, I said to him, "Didn't I tell you I don't fuck around, nigga? You must have me confused with another muthafucka." He remained silent as I continued my tirade. "Now you wanna tell me what you have me over here for?"

"Yeah Fee, I'll tell you what I want. I want you to work for me instead of Marcus. I need loyal soldiers on my team, and from what I understand, you're a big asset to his team," Ditto said, while he motioned Stone over and whispered something in his ear.

I replied, "I'm flattered that you would want me to join you at the table, but my loyalty is with Marcus."

He then stated with a little more purpose as Stone dragged Carla out of the room. "Yeah, but with Marcus, you'll always be under him. I could give you your own crew and put you on top. The money you make with him is pennies compared to what you'll make with me."

I cut him off and said, "It ain't about the money. Marcus is like a brother to me and can't shit come between that, so I'm gonna have to pass on that offer."

He nodded his head and said, "Alright then, I can respect that. No hard feelings here." I turned to walk away and he stopped and said, "Feelow, we don't need to let Marcus know about this. So, let's just keep it between us."

***

I was shocked when Feelow took the crack filled pipe from Carla and threw it against the wall. I really thought I had been given the correct information on him and decided to handle the nigga that gave it to me. “Yo, bring that bitch back in here,” I said to Stone, and he immediately left the room to get Carla.

She was still naked when he brought her back in with me, and I knew she was still mad about her pipe. “Come on over here and smoke on this pipe,” I said as I once again pulled my dick out.

Not wanting to see my wood, Stone turned his head a bit. Carla hesitated to follow my command. When Stone peeped her reluctance, he walked up behind her and pushed her forward. Carla dropped to her knees and pulled me in. I looked up at Stone as Carla deep throated my monster and said, “Stay on point at all times because if he tells Marcus, we may have a problem on our hands. Oh yeah and bring me the nigga who fed me that information.” Stone nodded his head just as my cum shot down Carla’s throat.

***

I couldn’t believe that Ditto had the nerve to think I would betray Marcus like that. The lie I told to Marcus about where I was going had already weighed me down, so I knew not to dig my hole any deeper. I wasn’t sure if Ditto really knew about my habit or not. He may have just been testing the waters, but there was no way I’d let him in on my deepest secret. However, my mind started to wonder if Marcus had tipped him off in some way to test me, but why would Marcus do that to me? I had never given him reason. When Carla melted that rock on the pipe, my mouth watered and as bad as I wanted to put it to my lips, I just couldn’t do it. However, I knew I had that wake up waiting for me when I got home and although, I knew I should have driven to the bottom and made that pick up for Marcus, I drove home to suck on that glass dick instead.

When I got there, everything was just as I left it. I hurriedly took off all my clothes and sat on the edge of the bed. My dick hung low between my spread legs, but as soon as I inhaled, it began to harden. I had always been told that crack robbed men of their hardness, but it had the opposite effect on me. My dick would get rock hard and I would have to jack it off to relieve the pressure. It had been a while since I been up in some pussy because I had a hard time getting up without a hit. The last thing I needed was for a bitch to know what I did. However, I was about to make an exception, so I called someone who had been on my jock for the longest. I was going to smoke as much as I could until they got there, and then I was going to fuck until I was satisfied.

***

As soon as the words left her mouth, I pulled her into me. Her lips were soft against mine and as our tongues danced together, I could tell she was telling the truth about her innocence. The thought of being her first made me feel like a winner. All the bitches I'd fucked never meant shit to me and I'd always put my mind in beast mode before I went in, but I wanted to be gentle with her.

The tightness of her made me drive slowly at first. When she loosened up, I moved in and out of her a little faster. "Oh Marcus, it hurts, but it feels good at the same time," she cried out to me as our bodies connected.

"Damn Krystal, this pussy feels good. Shit," I said in pleasure and then stopped and told her to get on top. "Come on baby, I want you to ride this dick like you own it."

She looked at me innocently and asked, "What if I don't do it right?"

I kissed her lips and said, "Don't worry. You got this. Ride it and make it yours. Make yo' nigga feel good."

***

I thought the length and size of him would bust me open, but I was willing to take it just to be closer to him. I knew when he left after that call he had went to another woman. I felt it all in my spirit. I wanted to make sure it didn't happen again, so I gave him my virginity to show him that he didn't have to go anywhere else. I had never felt anything so good in my life and from that very first stroke, I was hooked. I knew from that moment on I would do anything for him. Anything.

***

Krystal had given me the most sacred thing a woman possessed and I knew I had her right where I wanted her. I needed a bitch on my team, so I could get to the big dogs. A takeover was going to come soon and when it did, Krystal would play a big part in helping me infiltrate it. The one thing a man couldn't resist was pussy. Even the strongest of bosses went weak from a woman's sex appeal and Krystal was very strong even though she didn't know it yet, and she was going to come in handy.

My mind shifted from pussy beside me to the nigga I trusted the most. I sat up, reached for my phone, and dialed Feelow's number and this time he answered. "Yo my man, what's good?" he said into the phone and I could have sworn I heard a female moaning in the background.

"Sound like you over there in some pussy," I said and then asked, "Aye, I hate to disturb you, but did you handle that bottom shit for me?'

"Yeah. Yeah, dawg. I did, but the pussy was so damn good that I brought it home with me. Let me finish wetting my dick up and I'll come drop it by you," Feelow said as the lie came easily off his tongue.

"Nah Fee, don't worry about it. I can swing by your crib while I'm out and pick it up. Save you a trip," I stated in a calm tone, so I wouldn't raise alarm.

"Uh. Well, um. As soon as I get this nut off, I'll be leaving out so I'll come to you. Save your gas, bro. Go 'head home. I'll be there within the next hour," he said nervously.

I decided to go along with what he said so he wouldn't be suspicious, "Aiight, Fee. I'll be there waiting on you. Peace out." I didn't know what was up with Feelow and as my heart sped up, I felt Krystal's arms around me. I moved them and stood up to face her and said, "Put some clothes on. You going with me this time."

***

I could tell that the phone call once again upset him so when he told me to get dressed, I didn't waste a second doing so. I didn't have any clothes and didn't want to put the same clothes back on, so I put on a pair of Marcus' sweatpants and a T-shirt. When he saw me, he shrugged and said, "Don't worry, Ma. I'ma take you shopping for some fresh threads."

***

I had never worried about Feelow doing me dirty, but I knew that something was going on with him and I wouldn't leave his place until I found out. I knew I shouldn't have brought Krystal, but if she wanted to be my bitch then she was gonna have to get use to stuff like this. I said to her as I drove to our destination, "My boy has a bitch with him so if I need you to handle her, you got me?"

She looked at me lustfully and said, "Til My Casket Drops."

***

I didn't pull in front of Feelow's complex because I didn't want to take the chance of him looking out the window and seeing me there. Me and Krystal got out and walked to his building and when I saw that his car was still there, I got more pissed off with each step. Feelow had always been able to keep his habit under control, but at that moment, I hoped that it was only the pipe that had made him lie to me. I didn't want to think that it could be anything else because I had real love for the boy. When we made it to his door, I told Krystal to knock. I knew that now that she'd cleaned up, he wouldn't recognize her and I hoped she didn't recognize him either. I knew if he saw me, he may have gotten spooked, so I had to use her for this mission.

***

I didn't mind knocking on the person's door if that's what Marcus wanted. I was going to show him that although I was white, I could ride with the best of them. I wasn't sure why he didn't want to knock himself, but I wasn't going to ask any questions. My momma always told me to never question a man because I may get an answer that would break my heart. She said that sometimes it's just best not to know. Marcus stood to the side as I knocked lightly and then he said in an irritated voice, "Damn, girl. Put some music behind that shit." I did as he said and a minute later, I heard the locks being undone.

Chapter Nine

I was deep in that ass when I heard a knock at my door. "Nah nigga, don't pull it out. That shit is starting to feel good," the person in front of me said as I put in that long stroke.

However, I pulled out anyway and stated, "Just keep that ass open. This won't take, but a minute." I walked out of my room without putting anything over my nakedness and went to answer my front door. When I looked out the peep hole, I saw a white girl and instantly got nervous because I didn't know any white bitches. I grabbed my gun off the side of the table before I undid my locks. She gasped and her eyes widened as I pointed the pistol between her eyes and asked, "Who the fuck are you and what are you doing at my door?"

Her answer was one I didn't expect, "Mmm, Mmm, Mmm," she said as she looked down at my dick and then continued, "I'll be whoever you want me to be if you promise to push that pipe up in me just right." I was thrown off by her answer but lowered my gun and stepped back anyway and when I did, another figure appeared.

***

Krystal didn't even flinch when Feelow's gun touched between her eyes. She gasped but took that shit like a champ which told me that the bitch was built for this shit. My dick instantly got hard, but her reward would have to wait until later. When Fee lowered his gun, I pushed my girl to the side and showed my face.

"What's up, my nigga? I was in the neighborhood so I thought I'd go ahead and stop by and pick up that paper," I said as his bare dick shriveled up between his thighs.

"Marcus, um, um well uh," he stuttered while he thought of another lie to tell me. His next words were another strike against him. "I got it down in the trunk of my car, so let me slide something on, and I'll go get it for you."

At the same time the lie rolled off his tongue, thunder rolled through the sky. He jumped at the sound of it so I asked him, "Why you so jumpy, Fee? You acting a little guilty of something."

"Nah, my man, nah, I'm just. I'm gonna go slide on some pants so I can go get that," he said in a shaky voice."

I responded, "Yeah, you already said that, but you still ain't moved. Nigga, I'm tired of looking at your dick so go handle that."

He looked from me to Krystal and then back at me before asking, "What's up with the white girl here? Bitch looks familiar."

"Yeah, well, I ain't here to discuss her. Nigga, where my bread at?" I said as I moved closer to him.

As soon as I got up on him, another nigga appeared and said, "Damn Fee, my ass in here waiting on that good dick. What's taking you so .....?" When he laid eyes on me, he cut his sentence short.

"What the fuck? Nigga, you gay?" I asked Feelow.

He hung his head low and said, "Nah, man. I just… I just like it sometimes. I never wanted you to find out."

I took a step back and then turned to Krystal and said, "Go back to the car and wait for me." I threw the keys to her and stated, "I hope your white ass can drive." I waited until she walked out before I finished my business with Feelow. "Yo dawg, I know you lied to me earlier about where you was going and you lying to me now because I've already been to the bottom." I softened my voice up because no matter what, I had love for the nigga in front of me. "What's up with you, man? You ain't never lied to me before."

Feelow picked up a pair of shorts he had lying on the arm of the sofa and sent the other nigga back to the room before he answered me, "I don't know, man. I was about to take my wake up and my phone rang. It was Ditto asking me to pull through and see him." He swallowed hard before he continued, "When I got there he had Crackhead Carla sucking his nuts and shit and then handed her a piece to put on the pipe for me and as bad as I wanted to hit that bitch, I just couldn't do it."

From the look in his eyes, I knew that he was telling me the truth. I didn't interrupt him and listened as he finished. "I don't know how he knew I did that shit or why if he didn't know, what made him test me like that? I told him that I didn't get down like that, and then asked him why he called me instead of you. He then offered me a job with him talking about I'm only getting pennies with you, but I turned that shit down. His eyes watered as he continued, "Man, I ain't gonna lie, but I thought you was in on that shit. Like you was testing my loyalty and shit. It had me fucked up in the head that's why I ignored your calls and lied to you about where I was going. I'm sorry, man. I should have known better. I'm sorry."

I sat down so I could process all of what Feelow just told me. Not only did he lie to me twice, but I found out he liked dick. That was a lot to take in and had my head spinning. I put my hands in the praying position and rubbed them together. "Man, say something," he stated in an irritated voice.

I looked at him and then stood back up and said, "We gonna keep it moving like you didn't just tell me all of this. I'm gonna have to act normal around D and I need you to do the same when you with me. When the time is right, we gonna take that nigga all the way out."

Feelow nodded his head in agreement and then asked, "Yo Marcus, what up with that white bitch? She looked real familiar."

I smiled at the thought of her because I felt like I had found me a real-life Bonnie and said to my nigga, "That's the bitch from the alley. I don't think she recognized you."

"Damn, man. Bitch cleaned up nice. I mean, I do still like pussy too," he said as he let out a small chuckle.

"Nah nigga, stand down. I'm keeping that one," I said with a smile.

"What? Don't let me find out that little dirty ass white girl got you sprung already," he said with a concerned look.

I grabbed the mound in my pants and said, "This right here was her first, and man, you know I put that work in." I paused and then continued, "But, I ain't found a pussy yet that can tame this beast."

We shared a laugh and gave each other dap and when another voice interrupted our brotherhood bonding, all laughter stopped. "Yo nigga, you coming to finish what you started or what?" I looked the black motherfucker in his eyes and if looks could kill, he would have fell out then. Feelow didn't respond to him but looked at me instead. The disappointment showed in my eyes, but him getting dick wasn't enough to break apart what we had.

"Go ahead, my brotha. We'll talk about that another time," I said as I pulled him in for a man hug and walked out.

The cool air felt good against my skin but wasn't enough to tame the fire that burned my soul. I couldn't believe that Ditto would try my hand like that. I heard someone call my name and break me from my thoughts. When I stopped walking and turned to see who it was, I saw a big dude come walking across the parking lot. Although, he looked familiar I put my hand on the gat that was tucked in my waist. When he got closer, I let the gat go and reached out to shake his hand.

"What's up, Tyck? Nigga, when you got out?" I asked with a smile. Tyckori Wallace had been sent away when he was fifteen years old for a robbery he was involved in. Since he played the smallest part and had never been in trouble before, he would only be gone until his twenty-first birthday.

"I just got out two days ago, man. It's good to see you doing bigger and better things. What's up? Put a nigga on," he said.

I laughed and said, "Man, you sure you ready for this life?"

"Yeah, man. I gotta get my paper up, so I can move into my own shit. I love my sister and all, but she ask too many damn questions. Man, I ain't been home, but two days and three different niggas done been up in that bitch." He shook his head in disappointment and added, "I mean, I know that's my flesh and blood, but Tykita been a ho since she was in diapers. What can I say?" He shrugged his shoulders.

I laughed at his words and told him, "Come on, Tyck. Follow me."

We talked it up while we walked to my car and when Krystal saw me, she got out. I looked at her pretty ass and then introduced her to Tyck.

"Dayum Marcus, you putting vanilla cream in your coffee now. I never thought I'd see the day. And she fine," he stated.

"Back up, nigga. That white bitch is about that life and will bust a cap in your ass," I said, so he would know not to try me or her. I reached in the car and pulled five bands out of the bag I had in the back seat and handed them to him and said, "I'll hit you up later on with some work, but here's a little gwap to get you started."

His face lit up as he said, "Thanks, man. I'll be ready when you are." We gave each other dap before he walked away and then me and Krystal got back in the car and drove away.

I lived on the same block as the twins Tyckori and TyKita growing up and had a boyhood crush on their mom. I swore that one day I would marry her. I use to tease Tyck by telling him he'd be calling me daddy. His twin sister would be on my jock hard and would tell me, "Put that pipe in me right, and you can be my daddy without marrying her ass." I was only ten years old when she told me that and at age twelve I gave into her. I spent the night at their house and when everyone else went to sleep, TyKita and I snuck out and went to the tree house in their backyard.

My dick was big for a twelve-year-old, but TyKita sucked it with all her might and gave me my first orgasm. She swallowed my cum and all, and after that night I swore I was a man and tried to holler at her momma but she shot me down before I could get all the words out, of my mouth. I walked into her kitchen one day and the sight of her fat ass gave me an instant hard on, so I grabbed a hold of it and stood beside her and said, "Aye yo, Ms Wallace wit yo fine ass. Let a little nigga get some play. I got that ......" and then she shut me up.

"You got that what? Look lil nigga, you ain't got enough dick to fill this grown woman pussy up, so you come back and see me when you grow a few more inches longer. By the way, I don't fuck little boys so when you grow into them little nuts of yours, come and smell me then." Then she walked out. I was going to hold her to her word, but by the time I was legal she found out she caught HIV from one of her exes, so I kept my dick at bay.

I reminisced on the good days and while deep in thought I felt someone touch my arm breaking me out of my daydream. I then heard Krystal's voice, "Marcus! Marcus, we're back. Are you okay?"

I shook it off and answered her, "Yeah, I just- I was just thinking about the good ole' days when shit was right in my life. I'm good." We got out of my ride and walked to the door of the condo. I pushed my hand down in the sweats she had on and rubbed on her clit and said, "Go in and get my pussy ready while I make this run. I'ma see if you really taste like vanilla cream when I get back."

I kissed her pretty lips and then pulled my hand out as she said, "Be careful, Marcus. I'll have her open and ready when you make it back."

I smiled and turned to walk away. I made it a few steps and then turned back to her and said, "Krystal."

She turned in my direction, "Yes, Marcus?'

"You did good today." Then I got back in my ride and pulled off.

Chapter Ten

Reality didn't set in until the steel door shut in myface.What had I done? I'd convinced myself that Marcus would reach out to me. How could he not? We had been through the mud together and since I always had his back, I just knew that he would have mine too.

The small cell consisted of a steel toilet and sink, along with a small wall locker. The only place to sit was a flat mattress laid out on a slab of steel attached to the wall. I had seen television shows about jail and didn't remember it looking like that. I didn't even bother to make up the mattress, but instead just lied down and covered up with a sheet. I was exhausted, but still, it took hours for me to fall asleep. When I finally did, my dreams invaded my mind.

"Nigga, you asked for this," Marcus said as he kicked the man in the head with the tip of his steel toed boot. Whop! Whop! I felt the blood as it spattered on my face but was too in shock to wipe it off. Whop!

"Ugh, please don't kill me man, please." He begged for his life, but there would be no mercy for him. He had committed the ultimate crime and would now pay for it. "You, Muthafucka." Whop! Whop! Marcus continued to kick as the blood flowed out. He begged for his life once more, "Please, Marcus. I'm sorry, man. Please." His cries became less and less until they finally stopped for good.

"Muthafucka, you made me do this shit." Marcus then pulled out his gun and put a bullet between the man's eyes.

Morning came without a warning and the sun shined bright through the small window. I could hear movement outside my door and got up to look out of the bars that lined a small square of it. Two women walked up to me. One looked at me like I had a disease. I asked, "Hey, excuse me, but could you tell me what's going on?"

She laughed in my face and said, "You must be the dumb white bitch who copped that murder yo' nigga did? Bitch, you better learn that niggas move on to the next one when we away. He's deep in another pussy right now and look at you. Don't even have a damn clue." She shook her head and they walked away, leaving me as I stood there and felt another piece of my heart shatter.

My heart pounded harder and faster than it ever had before when I was led into the same courtroom I had been acquitted in. The handcuffs and shackles were tight around my wrists and ankles. The spectators looked right at me when I walked in, but I wasn't concerned with their prying eyes, because my eyes searched for Marcus. However, he was nowhere to be found.

I knew they would question me about the events that took place the night of the killing. I wanted to just plea out, but the public defender said to go to trial and claim self-defense in hopes of getting out of it. The prosecutor was happy about that because he wanted to hear me tell the story, hoping I would slip and he could catch me in a lie, but I knew and remembered every single detail.

The badgering gave me a headache, but no matter what question I was asked I stood strong and was on point with my answers. "Miss Madison, how did you know the victim and what type of relationship did you have with him?" The prosecutor was a short chubby white man with a gap between his teeth that caused some of his words to come out with a whistling sound. He stared deep into my eyes as if he could see straight through me, but I was white, not transparent.

I answered, "I was walking down Fair Street on my way to the store, and he snatched me up. I had never seen him before so we never had any type of relationship."

He cleared his throat before he asked the next question, "How did someone as small as you overpower someone of his stature?"

In my mental, I saw Marcus pick up the lead pipe and knock him to his knees before he started with the kicks. I knew my story had to be viable, so they would believe it so I stated in a serious tone, "He…He bent over to take off his shoes, and I hit him in the head with a pipe that I saw lying on the ground. Once he was down, I proceeded to kick him in the head with the tip of my heels." I stopped and took a deep breath before I continued," There was blood everywhere and I thought I'd killed him, but as I turned to walk away he grabbed my ankle and pulled me down. That's when I saw his gun."

The prosecutor then asked, "And where was his gun, Miss Madison?"

His beady little eyes looked at me vengefully, but I kept on my poker face and answered him," His gun was on the ground beside him. When I saw it, I picked it up and shot him between the eyes. He left me no choice. It was me or him."

The trial lasted longer than I expected and they continued to ask the same questions over and over and over hoping to catch a flaw in my story. Had I not been with Marcus when it happened, they would have charged me with perjury. I had to believe because I refused to let Marcus sit where I had sat while the white man questioned him and secretly wished to hang another young black man. I wouldn't allow it to happen, especially to the one I was in love with.

All of a sudden the courtroom door opened and a black woman I had never seen walked in and screamed at me, "Bitch, tell the fucking truth. That nigga don't give a fuck about you. Look around, that bastard don't even have the decency to show up and support your lie."

"Order in the court!" the judge hollered while he beat his gavel on the hard wood in front of him.

However, the lady continued to scream and get closer to me, "Stop being a dumb bitch and make that motherfucker pay for what he did."

The bailiff grabbed her before she could get any closer, but it didn't stop the wrath that she was spewing, "I saw it all, bitch. Tell the truth and make his ass pay. Tell the fucking truth." Another bailiff came and escorted me out of the courtroom until they could calm the woman down. Her words hit me hard because there was no way she could have known what happened that night unless she was there too. I thought hard and tried to remember every single detail…and then it hit me.

Chapter Eleven

I could see the disappointment in Marcus' eyes when Jay walked back out of the bedroom, but he didn't want to waste his words talking about it. Jay was a major dealer from out of Miami and we had met when I'd made a run down there for a pickup. When we looked into each other's eyes, we had a connection and had been meeting up when either of us would be in the other's city.

I didn't consider myself gay because I still liked pussy too and could get it from any bitch I pulled up on. However, I enjoyed a good dick just as much. After Jay and I finished our rendezvous, he left, and I hopped in the shower to rinse off the sin I had just committed. No sooner than I jumped out my cell rang, "Fee, this Trap. I'm outta gas and need you to swing by with five gallons to put in my tank," Trap said desperately into the phone.

I could hear his system bumping in the background and said, "Aiight, nigga. I just stepped out of the shower so give me a minute."

"Aiight, I'll be waiting. Peace," Trap stated before the phone went dead.

I finished drying off and sat on the end of my bed, so I could fix me up a nice hit before I went on the mission. I put the tan colored rock on the pipe and lit it. The sizzling sound it made when it melted made my dick rise to attention. I had wished that Jay was still there so he could stroke it while I inhaled my poison, but he didn't know about my habit either. I told myself while I held the smoke in my lungs that I was going to give that shit up. I had smoked long enough, and although I enjoyed its pleasure, it was time to let it go. I wondered if my dick would still get hard without it since I had depended on it for so long. There would be only one way to find out, and as soon as I delivered that package to Trap, I had every intention of getting my answer.

When I pulled up to the bottom Trap met me at the door, and we gave each other dap. "What's up, nigga?" he asked. "You good?" he asked and then moved out of the way, so I could get inside.

I answered, "Yeah man, shit sweet. What's up with you?" Creep then came out of the back room with his dick swinging and saw me. He fixed himself, tucking his member inside his drawers, showing me the proper respect.

"Yo, Fee. Nigga, it's good to see you, my man," he said while he held his hand out for some dap.

I shook my head and pulled away and said, "Bitch, I don't know where that muthafucka have been at."

"Shit nigga, this muthafucka was deep in yo' mama's pussy last night," he said with a laugh.

"Nigga, you know those mama jokes will get ya ass slumped up in here."

"I'm just fuckin' wit' you, bro. Let me go get dressed."

Before he made it all the way out of the room, Netta walked in with a short t-shirt on. Her ass cheeks could be seen peeking out from the bottom. She walked up on Creek, put her hand around his dick, and started stroking it. She didn't even stop when I spoke up, "Yo Netta, what the fuck you doing? Bitch, Milo gonna kill yo ass."

She rolled her neck, but never let go of the dick and said with an attitude, "Fuck Milo. I ain't seen that nigga in days and a bitch got needs. He probably laid up with yo' bitch somewhere."

She then put her arms around Creep's neck and while he lifted up the t-shirt, he put a hand on each ass cheek. He spread her ass open and said, "Yo Fee, you wanna hit this ass while I beat the pussy up."

I really didn't give a fuck about Netta, but Milo was my boy. I shook my head and asked her, "Bitch, where the fuck Lil Milo at?"

She smacked her tongue in her mouth and said, "That lil nigga wit my neighbor. He good. He ain't yo' son, so don't worry about his bad ass." She looked back at Creep and smiled before she stared hungrily. "Come on nigga, let a bitch guide this dick where it should be. I wanna feel this shit up in my intestines." She looked back at me and said, "You can get it too, Feelow. I bet you got some of that good come back dick."

I didn't respond as her and Creep left the room. When they were gone, I turned back to Trap and said, "Yo dawg, lets handle this business so I can get the fuck outta here."

Trap said, "Hold on, man. Let me make this quick call." When Trap came back in the room, I passed him the five kilos he'd asked for and looked at him suspiciously. He asked, "Nigga, why you looking at me like that?"

"Trap, quit playing," and then asked, "Nigga, where that money at?"

"Yo man, Marcus already swooped by since you didn't show up when you were supposed to," he said with his head cocked to the side. I didn't even respond because Trap shouldn't have known my business like that. I wondered what else Marcus had told him about me. I instantly became paranoid and asked, "Did you just call Marcus, nigga?" he asked. "Yeah, that's a problem."

I didn't want to reveal how I really felt, so I brushed it to the side, "Nah, man. You know that's my brotha. I just don't like for y'all bitches to know when I'm moving."

He looked at me sideways and said, "Man, I ain't no bitch and I'ma let that shit slide. I was told to call Marcus when yo black ass showed up so you check him with that shit, nigga. I don't owe you no damn explanation." I stared at him for a minute and then turned to walk out. I could hear Netta moaning and telling Creep to fuck her harder and then I slammed the door behind me.

***

I immediately called Marcus back as soon as Feelow left out, "Yo man, you better check yo' bitch ass brother before I bust a cap in his ass. Muthafucka wanna call himself checking me and shit," I said, with anger in my voice.

"What the fuck you talking about, Trap?" Marcus asked agitated.

"Nigga acted like it was a problem with me calling you, but unlike his fuck ass I do what the fuck I'm told. So, no disrespect to you, dawg, but if it happens again, I'm gonna put something hot in that ass." I seemed to get angrier with each word I spewed out.

When I calmed down Marcus asked, "Did he bring you the five gallons of gas you needed so you can start your car back up?"

I answered in a mild chilled voice, "Yeah man, thanks. I'm actually about to go get in my ride right now. I'll hit you up later man, Peace." Then the call disconnected.

***

I thought about what Trap told me and would question Feelow about it when the time was right. I had already felt the change in him, but brushed it off, but now I had to check him about the next nigga. Trap and Creep had been with me from day one and I never had a problem with my money or my product, so I couldn't allow anyone else to fuck that up. Not even my right had man. However, I had to handle some business with Ditto first.

When I pulled up to our meeting place, I had to get my mind together before I went in because I didn't want him to know that Feelow had told me what happened. I couldn't hide my anger very well but knew that I had to until I figured everything out. I had already made a call to a new connect out of Baltimore that I had met through Milo. I had already told him of Milo's demise and he understood without retaliation. I knew eventually that Netta would also hear of the news.

I didn't even get a chance to knock on the door before Stone opened it and stood there with a somber look on his face like he always did. I said to him when I entered, "Nigga, you need to get out of Ditto's ass and get you some pussy so you can smile."

He didn't respond nor did his look change when he slammed the door behind me. I shook my head and walked to the back of the house where I found Ditto in the hot tub with two naked red bitches. When he saw me, he said, "Marcus, get undressed and join me. There's plenty of pussy here for the both of us." The two women giggled and looked at me as they anticipated my next move. I guess

I didn't move quick enough because one of them got out and walked over to me.

When she was right up on me, she grabbed the bottom of my shirt and attempted to pull it up, but I pushed her hand away and said, "Nah, I'm good. My bitch ain't leave nothing for nobody else."

Ditto said, "What's up, nigga. You got you some white pussy and feel like you too good for some dark meat. That white bitch got you sprung already?" The girl shrugged and walked back to the hot tub when I didn't answer him. I watched her bare ass jiggle and almost changed my mind, but I really wasn't in the mood to play in pussy. Ditto noticed the look on my face and said to the woman, "Excuse me ladies, but I gotta handle this business. Keep each other entertained until I get back." He got out, grabbed a towel to wrap around his waist, and said to me, "Let's go inside."

Ditto fixed himself a drink and offered me one, but I declined. I wanted a clear head for the conversation. After he got his drink, he sat down, adjusted the towel to cover his dick, then looked at Stone, and said, "Yo man, why don't you go out there to them bitches and get you some pussy, shoot a load off and chill." Stone smiled, but still said nothing and left the room. When he was gone, Ditto immediately began to ask questions, "So, what's on your mind, Marcus? You seem uptight. I hope we don't have an arising issue." I looked at him sideways because I knew what he was talking about, but I had to keep cool and play dumb.

"I'm not sure what you mean, so I'm just gonna let you know why I'm here," I said as he looked at me. "Look man, you picked me up when I was at my worst and made me somebody. I'm who I am today because of you and I appreciate it, but I'm ready to venture out on my own and set up my own shit."

He took a sip of the brown liquid that was in his glass and said, "Well Marcus, I thought you was on your own. You only come to me for product. So, I'm not getting what you're telling me here."

I knew I had to put it all out there so I did, "I'm not gonna be working for you or taking orders from you no more. I'll be getting my product elsewhere and I'll be the one giving orders. I won't be reporting to anyone else and all the money delivered to me will be mine."

Ditto emptied his glass and rose from the chair he sat in. He went back to the mini bar and poured another drink before he came and sat back down. "So, you just gonna take your money to another supplier and cut me all the way out, after all I've done for you, nigga?" He emptied his glass again before he came over and stood in front of me in an intimidating stance.

I looked up at him and said, "I told you when I started that I wouldn't be here for long. I learned from the best, Ditto. You were a good teacher, but I'm ready to run my own shit."

He laughed and said as he looked in my eyes, "Nigga, you go up in some white pussy and now you think you ready to run the world. I knew I should have fucked that white bitch while I had her in my possession."

I immediately stood up in his face and said in an angry voice, "Leave the white girl out of this. She ain't got shit to do with it."

He lifted his eyebrows and stated, "Sounds like the little white bitch got you in your feelings. Let me find out that's your weakness. Get the fuck outta my face. You quit working for me when I tell you to."

I shook my head because honestly, I wasn't scared of Ditto and I knew that half of his set would stand behind me on this move. I decided I'd let my crew recruit them onto our team before I came back to take his shit all the way over. "Yeah. Whatever, man. I'll bring you the rest of what I owe you and then we're done." I walked out and knew that once I completely pulled away, I could very well have a war to fight. I would be ready for whatever Ditto brought my way.

Ditto talked to his crew like shit and treated them like they were beneath him so I knew pulling them would be easy. In the drug world, it was all about respect and loyalty. Those two things came hand in hand. I respected all of his workers while he fucked their bitches and paid them little. Niggas was having hard times taking care of their seeds with the little money he paid them, but I would change all that. I decided to wait until the next day to go back and see Feelow because I wanted to go home. I could run up in something warm. After that, I would plan a trip to Augusta to see a gun runner. I knew I would need some heavy artillery to win the battle I would eventually have with Ditto.

Chapter Twelve

When I left from dropping off the package to Trap, I felt some kind of way. My paranoia rose from the thought of Marcus checking up behind me. We had been friends a long time and he had never done anything like that before. It made me feel like he really did set up that whole thing with Ditto just to check my loyalty. Since Marcus wanted to try me like that, I decided I may as well give him more of a reason to do so. I had a couple of niggas I fucked with through Jay that wouldn't mind coming up and getting some territory. I would get my plan together first and then contact them to help me pull it together.

I hadn't smoked any dope since that morning and I had it in my mind to get off the pipe. I figured that I could do it since I'd never let it get the best of me. However, I told myself I would take just one more hit and then I'd really quit.

***

I knew from what I'd just told Ditto that he would treat me different from that day on, but I wouldn't let that affect me. I respected him enough to let him know so I felt like he should have respected my decision. The money I made him would only put a small dent in my pocket, but I saw that nigga was greedy and that alone would get him cased up. I had already planted my seed so I knew I had to move full speed ahead.

I pulled up to my condo and got out as I thought about the issues I would face. Those thoughts quickly left my mind as soon as I walked into my bedroom. My dick got hard as soon as I saw her. I immediately undressed and crawled in beside her. "Mmm. I been waiting on you," she said with a smile on her pretty face.

I kissed her cheek and said as I tugged on the t-shirt she had covering her, "Take this shirt off so that a nigga can dress you with his tongue." The white girl changed something in me in just a matter of days.

I knew I needed to snap out of it so I could focus. I knew if I didn't that, she could easily blur my vision and get me and her both killed. Ditto would already be planning his revenge so I needed to be a step ahead of him. I would school Krystal on what was about to go down right after I taught her how to suck my dick.

***

"Damn Keisha, a bitch ain't neva sucked my nuts like that," I said as she covered my balls with her lips one at a time. After I took what was supposed to be my last hit, my dick felt like it would burst. I rode the stroll, came across Keisha, and picked her up to curb my appetite.

"You like that, Feelow?" she asked right before she stuck the tip of her tongue in my asshole not knowing that it was the ultimate treat for me.

I told her, "Move that tongue and push one of them fingers up in that bitch for me." Keisha didn't hesitate and as soon as she slid not one, but two fingers inside of me, I came.

"Damn, Feelow. How you gonna cum and you ain't even gave me the dick yet? Nigga, this pussy wants to cum too," she said with a quick head roll.

I breathed heavily and said, "Just give me a minute to take a piss and I'ma fuck the shit out of your ass." I hadn't only picked up Keisha to get my nut off, but also because I knew she had a vendetta against Marcus. The last time they were together, he treated her like shit. She wanted to be claimed by a baller, but she fucked too many niggas for anyone to want her as their main bitch. However, I knew that ho was scandalous and I was gonna use her to help me bring Marcus and Ditto down. When she served her purpose, I would serve her back to the nigga before me.

I went in the bathroom and sat on the toilet before I placed a hit on my pipe. I continued to tell myself that I would be the last one. As the dope melted and the smoke filled my lungs, Keisha walked in. "Oh my GOD, Feelow. I am so sorry. The door was unlocked." I blew out a cloud of smoke after she busted me and knew what I had to do. "Come on in, Keisha. Come sit on this dick." She looked like she was still in shock at the revelation she had discovered but did as I said. She turned her fat ass to me and spread her legs open. When I pulled her down to me by the hips, my dick slid into her with ease.

I said, "I want you to be my girl, Keisha. You up for that?"

She moaned in pleasure, "Yes, Feelow. Ah, shit. Yeah. Hell, yeah. I'll be yours. Damn, this dick is good. Fuck!" I wanted her to stay mad at Marcus, so my plan would come together better. So I said as I hit her a long stroke, "Marcus don't know how to appreciate a bitch like you, huh?"

"Uhh, Uhh," she grunted as she winded her hips in a circular motion.

"Nigga gonna lose out, but I'ma make you mine and together we gonna shut his bitch ass down. How you like that, Keisha?" I asked as her pussy juice coated my dick.

She came up off the dick and said, "I like the sound of that, Feelow. I owe that nigga for treating me like a trick bitch. Like I wasn't good enough for his ass. Fuck that nigga. Just tell me what I need to do." Then, I slid my dick in her ass.

***

I didn't know what was going on with Feelow and Marcus and really didn't give a fuck. His dick had me in a zone, and I would've agreed to do anything for him. The thought of him wanting me to be his girl had my pussy wetter than it had ever been. I had been wanting to be claimed by a baller and Feelow was doing his thing in the streets. Even though he worked for Marcus, he still had major status in all the hoods. However, I was shocked when I walked in the bathroom and caught him smoking crack. If someone would have told me, I never would have believed it because he didn't carry himself like that. His dick was so damn good. It felt like it went deeper with each stroke. I played with my clit while I rode him and right when I was about to cum he stopped me.

***

"Come on Keisha, let's go back into the room. I want you to try this shit." He pushed me off his dick and my asshole continued to throb as if he were still inside of it. He stroked his length all the way back to the bed. I laid back on the pillow and spread my legs for him but was disappointed when he didn't climb on the bed with me. Instead, he pulled a plastic baggie out of his pants pocket, dumped the contents out on the table, and said, "Come on over here beside me." I looked at him in a confused manner but did what he said.

He pulled another chair in front of the one he sat in and told me to sit there. He picked up my legs and put one across each arm rest, so they would be open and then he put a piece of crack on his pipe. The sound of it being melted made me think of a piece of meat being laid down in hot grease. After he melted it, he reached over and put it to my lips. I pulled back and said, "Nah Feelow, I don't get high."

He looked me in the eyes and said, "You my bitch now, so you do what the fuck I tell you to do. Now bring them pretty lips here."

***

I needed to have full control of Keisha and I knew that my dick alone wouldn't work, although I knew my dick game was on point. I needed to use a little something extra, so I took out my dope and melted a piece on the pipe. When she pulled her head back, I got pissed off, but didn't let her know it. That bitch was gonna smoke that shit even if I had to hold her down and make her. After a few seconds, she grabbed the pipe and finally put her lips to it. I lit the end and said, "That's my girl. Yeah, baby. Daddy gonna fuck this pussy real good for you since you being such a good girl." I reached up and pinched one of her nipples really hard while she inhaled. When her lungs had pulled in as much as they could, she released the pipe from her hold and leaned her head back.

When she finally emptied the smoke from her lungs, she looked at me and asked, "Can I have another one?"

***

I had to give it to Marcus because the nigga had some balls if he thought I was just gonna let him start taking his money elsewhere. I went out back to where Stone was with the woman and dropped my towel. I needed to release some stress and pussy was the best medicine. When the one that was riding Stone's face saw me, she got up and came over to me and instantly dropped to her knees. When she pulled my dick into her warm mouth, I said, "Stay ready, Stone. I feel a war about to start." No sooner than I said it, I felt a presence behind me and turned around.

***

The way he looked in my eyes brought chills to my inner core and although my heart told me I shouldn't fear him, I still did. I saw his side kick Stone push the woman he had with him to the side and when he did, Ditto held his hand out to stop him from moving in too close to me and asked, "What the fuck did I tell you about coming to my house unannounced?" He had been disrespectful to me almost all of his life, but it got worse after I killed his father. He didn't care that I had to do it to save my own life.

His father Dittrick Senior and I had met when I was only fourteen. Dittrick was twenty-one and supplied the entire south with drugs. The first time we fucked, I became pregnant with Dittrick Junior or Ditto as his father would call him because he said that was his double. When my parents found out I was pregnant they pressed Dittrick to marry me or go to jail for statutory rape, but they really only wanted him to marry me so they wouldn't have to take care of me anymore and their threats worked.

Dittrick had no respect for me because he felt my parents stole his freedom to do what he wanted. He didn't want to be tied down to one female and marrying me wouldn't change that. He would bring other bitches up in the house and would fuck them in the same bed I laid in. The more he moaned and told the bitches it was their dick, the angrier I became. I would try to turn my back to them, but he would make me turn back over and watch as they swallowed his cum. He would say to me, "You see this, Delores? Now this is how you spose to suck a dick. Yeah bitch, make sure you swallow this cum." The tears would form in my eyes and instead of comforting me, he would tell me, "Don't worry, Dee. I'm about to make this bitch suck on that young pussy of yours so you can feel good, too." Then he would laugh.

His behavior lasted for years and even after I had his son, he would still bring bitches in the house. He started schooling Ditto to the game when he was only five years old. By the time Ditto was seven he could cook, cut and weigh drugs just as good as any other veteran in the game. At eight years old, Dittrick taught him how to shoot a gun and even allowed him to watch as he tortured disloyal workers. He even allowed Ditto to beat one to death with a hammer. When Ditto was twelve, Dittrick brought home two women and while one sucked his dick the other one taught Ditto all about sex. That first piece of pussy led to many more and I'd finally had enough.

"Dittrick, you're a piece of shit for allowing our son to sell dope and fuck random grown ass women. You fucking no good bastard. I'm tired of this shit!" I hollered at him.

Then he grabbed my neck and said, "Bitch, I pay the bills in this muthafucka and that is my son. You wanna start selling that pussy of yours and help pay some bills so you can run a little something? Huh? Shut yo ass up." He threw me on the ground and when he did I jumped up and started throwing fists at him, but he put a stop to it real quick and knocked me the fuck out.

When I woke up a strange nigga was between my legs eating my pussy as Dittrick and Ditto stood by and watched. When I tried to get up Dittrick came over to the bed with a belt, hit me across my bare chest with it, and said, "Bitch, lay yo ass there and give that nigga what he paid for."

I looked from him to our son and saw no mercy in either one of their eyes. I asked through tears, "Why are you doing this to me, Dittrick? And, in front of our son. You are wrong you bastard. I'm gonna pack my shit and take our son the fuck away from you."

As soon as I said it, Ditto walked up to the bed and stood beside his father and told the man between my legs, "That's enough, nigga." I let out a sigh of relief as he looked in my eyes and added, "Get up and push a dick in that bitch." Then him and his father laughed. Soon after that incident, I started getting high so I could deal with things a little easier. The abuse got worse when I'd had more than I could take. I waited until Dittrick was passed out one night and put the gun to his head. Because of the abuse I suffered at his hands and the hatred the police had for him, I got off on self-defense and had been under Ditto's hands ever since.

***

I pushed the bitch from off my dick and turned to the woman who birthed me. Her pleading eyes glared at me as she said, "Son, I'm going away to get clean. I don't wannna do this anymore. I was hoping that when I came back we could work on a real relationship. I love you, Dittrick. Regardless of anything that has happened. Please son, give me a chance to make things right."

He looked at me through the eyes of a killer and said as he made the woman in front of him bend over, "How you gonna make shit right, bitch? You can't bring my muthafuckin pops back. Shit, this pussy wet as fuck. Everybody knows once a crackhead always a crackhead. Matter of fact. Mmm… This pussy good." He continued to fuck the woman in front of him while he spoke to me. After a few more strokes he pulled out and continued his tirade, "Stone, give this bitch something to smoke and get her the fuck outta my face." Then he shot his cum all over the woman's back.

Chapter Thirteen

I fucked Krystal with so much passion that I almost fooled myself. I was under so much pressure because I had to deal with Feelow and his potential disloyalty and think about a war that I knew would ultimately begin. Krystal's pussy was so good that when I went in, I wouldn't think about anything else. Although, it felt nice when my mind was cleared of all that clutter, but I knew it wouldn't change anything.

I woke her up early so I could take her to get some fresh gear. While she checked out price tags, I checked out my surroundings. I felt like everyone looked at me sideways, but I knew it was only because of the conversation I'd had with Ditto. Once he realized I was serious, he would not hesitate to declare war, and I had to be ready when he struck.

***

I could tell that Marcus had a lot on his mind and wished that I could do something about it. When we had sex, he was more aggressive and although I liked his beast mode, I wanted his mind to be free. On the way back home from shopping I went against what my momma taught me and questioned him. "Marcus, what's going on with you?"

He looked over at me and responded, "It's nothing you need to worry about."

I lifted my brows and said, "Dammit Marcus, fucking let me in on this shit. I can handle it."

When he pulled into the driveway, he said, "You wanna be in on this shit. Aight then, you can be. Now take your white ass in the crib and put that shit up."

His response pissed me off and I said angrily, "Nigga, you got me up in this bitch cooking fucking cocaine and talking about me being a boss bitch in the streets beside you, but you wanna keep other shit a fucking secret. What the fuck?"

"You ain't ready for this life, Krystal. Act like a real fucking white girl and take yo ass in the house. Go crochet a fucking blanket or something,"he stated in a loud voice. I sat there for a minute and before I was able to get another sentence out he looked at me with empty eyes and said, "And I ain't gonna be too many more niggas to you, white girl. Get the fuck out. I got shit to do."

Something inside of me told me not to test him, so I opened the door and got out. I didn't even bother getting my purchases out of the back seat. He could give that shit to the next bitch he fucked for all I cared. I walked to the door of the house and turned my head to give Marcus one final look right before he pulled off.

***

I couldn't explain why I didn't let Krystal know about the shit that would be popping off in the street. I knew that she could handle it, but for some reason I didn't want her involved. I picked up my phone and dialed a number and when they answered, I said, "Yo C, call a meeting. I'm on my way." I showed up to the spot that me and my crew held meetings at and when I walked in I saw everyone, but Feelow present and asked, "Yo, ain't nobody tried to call Fee? He should be here, too."

C-John spoke up, "I tried to reach that nigga, but he didn't pick up." He paused and then asked, "You want me to try again."

I shook my head and said, "Nah, we gonna continue. I'll go by and see him when we done."

Micro spoke up,"Yo Marcus, you pulled me outta some wet pussy so I hope this shit is important."

"Nigga, anything I call you about is more important than some pussy. That's the problem now. You niggas are losing focus and people on our team are gonna suffer for it," I said and then looked to Datsun. "Nigga, you ain't pick up on the signs that Milo was hitting that shit? And I get word nigga was chipping off the product."

Datsun said, "Yo man. That nigga ain't never did no shit like that in front of me, so how was I supposed to know?"

Micro cut in, “Hey, I heard they found his ass in a garage truck. Word on the street is somebody slumped his ass.”

“Yeah, and I been hitting Netta ass every night ever since. That bitch got some good-” I cut Creep off before he said anything else.

“Yo nigga, respect Milo even though he ain’t with us no more. We ‘bout to have bigger shit to deal with.”

Blow spoke up and said, “Chill, Boss Man. We just trying to mellow the mood. Now tell us what’s up.”

I broke it all down for them. “As y’all know I been dealing with Ditto all this time because he is the nigga that put me on, but he on some different shit now.” I paused and looked around to make sure everyone was still focused on my words. “That nigga tried to get my right hand to switch out on us and join him independently, but being the loyal ass nigga that Feelow is, he turned him down.”

Corey cut me off and asked, “Yo, why that nigga ain’t present for this discussion?”

“Yeah, man. He always telling us to contact him before we call you, but his ass is ghost now. What the fuck?” Black chimed in.

I held my hand up and all chatter stopped. I lied for Feelow because I didn’t want the rest of the crew to lose respect for him. “Maybe he had to handle some other shit and can’t get to his phone until he’s done. I’ll reach out to him, so get off his dick.” I continued to tell them about the beef we were going to have with Ditto, “Anyway, I went and saw D to let him know that I wouldn’t be needing services anymore.”

Blow asked, “Man, where we gonna get our work from?”

I stated confidently, “I got a new source out of Northwest Baltimore and the nigga gonna give me the keys for eighteen instead of the twenty-two I pay Ditto.”

Creep asked, “Yeah, but is the shit gonna be as proper? We don’t want to lose customers. Nigga, I’m trying to keep living good.”

“Actually, the product will be even more potent. My new man gets his shit straight from the Colombians, and it ain’t got no cut on it. Ditto always cut his before he repackaged it and gave it to me, however, he never knew that I caught on to that shit," I said to my crew.

"Shit, he may have to cut on it, but them fiends still be begging for it. Especially them hoes. Nigga, I got a new bitch sucking my dick every day," Corey claimed.

I looked at them as they laughed at Corey's statement and then finished my speech, "Yeah, the fiends do still beg and shit, but with the product I'm going to be getting from this Baltimore cat the sales are going to triple. I just hope you niggas are ready to live like kings."

The room erupted in yeahs and high fives and them Micro asked, "That sounds good my man, but the question is, how did Ditto react when you told him? I'm sure his ass wasn't happy when you told him that shit. That rat bastard nasty as fuck. I can't wait to take a shit on his ass."

C-John said, "Yeah, that muthafucka treat his own damn momma like a piece of shit. She be out there sucking dick and all just to keep that pipe filled."

I held a hand up to stop their tirade and said, "Aiight, aiight calm down. Let me finish so we can get back home to our bitches and our niggas for those it applies to."

They laughed and shouted, "Man, fuck you! I like pussy only!"

"Man, kiss my ass Marcus."

"Bitch, I'll cut a nigga dick off if he try me."

"Aiight, calm down. I'm just fucking with y'all, but on the real, anybody who ain't down with the plan speak the fuck up now," I said as the room got quiet.

Micro asked, "Yo Marcus, ain't this gonna start a war with Ditto crew?'

I answered him, "Yeah, it is, but I'm hoping to get some of his niggas to join forces with us. I mean, he treats them like shit just like his momma. So honestly, I think with yall's help we could probably pull Paris, Montell, and Trip to battle with us. The rest of them niggas gonna have to be put to sleep. So y'all with me or what?"

"Hell, yeah!" Blow hollered.

"Fucking right," Datsun agreed.

"Damn right. I'm ready for them bitches. Bring it on!" Black hollered and fist pumped.

Micro asked, "Yo Marcus, what about artillery? We gonna need more than these nines to put them niggas on they ass."

I told them about the trip I would be taking to Augusta to meet up with a gun runner. A couple of them asked to take that ride with me, but I already had my passenger picked out.

***

I wanted so bad to be that ride or die bitch that Marcus needed by his side but had to figure out how to make him give me that chance. The other side of the streets always piqued my interest and made me wanna be a dope boy's chic. I didn't want to just be a piece of pussy one came home to. I wanted to have my nigga's back and be hands-on, and I'd be damned if Marcus didn't let me.

Chapter Fourteen

I told Keisha to masturbate for me while I put another hit on the pipe for her. I wanna see you make that pussy cum. You my bitch now, so do what a nigga says, "I said to her because she acted like it was a problem, but I knew this bitch was a freak and I wanted her to perform. I needed to make this bitch bow down to my every word and getting her hooked on the pipe would make it to where I could control her better.

"Come on, Feelow. Stop playing," she said while she halfway played with her clit, but her cries didn't flex me at all.

"Bitch, play with that muthafucking pussy like I said, and you can get whatever the fuck you want. If you can't handle that shit, let me know, and I'll find me a bitch who can!" I hollered at her. Then I softened up my tone a little. "Come on baby," I said as I pushed a finger inside of her. "Don't you wanna please yo' nigga?'

"Yes, Feelow," she moaned.

I felt her juices coat my finger and said, "Bitch, this is my pussy now and if I tell you to play with it, then that's just what the fuck I mean." I passed her the pipe and then dropped to my knees. "Now suck on this glass while daddy sucks on this pussy."

I ate Keisha like it was my last meal and let her enjoy the hit. When she exhaled, she put the pipe down on the table, placed both of her hands on the back of my head, and said, "Oh, Feelow. You gonna have a bitch sprung. Yes, Daddy. Yes. Mmm… I'm gonna cum. Yes!" She grinded her hips harder and a couple of minutes later she came all over my chin. She breathed heavily and held on to me until she was empty, and then I got up and sat on the edge of the bed with my dick sticking straight up.

She looked from my eyes to my dick, but said nothing so I said it for her, "Fix a hit on that pipe for daddy and then bring yo ass over here and suck on this dick." She immediately got up to do as I instructed. She passed me the pipe and jiggled my balls in her hand while my dick disappeared in her mouth. I filled my lungs to capacity with the drug and after I let go of the smoke, I said, "I'ma need you to suck on Marcus' dick, just like this while I creep up on his ass. Nigga getting too big for his boxers and you just the bitch I need to help me cut his ass back down to size." Then I came.

***

I never thought I'd see the day when I would become a crackhead, but that first hit Feelow gave me had me in a euphoric state of mind. I had always said that I'd never fall victim to the streets and would talk shit to them hoes that would be in the alleys doing whatever to get that next hit. Now look at my ass, on my knees as I begged Feelow for more. It didn't matter what he asked me to do because I knew I would do it.

He was on some type of get back shit with Marcus and to get that feeling the first hit gave me, I'd be on that same shit with him. Feelow and I stayed in the room for the next two days while his phone vibrated over and over. However, when he saw it was Marcus, he ignored it. My pussy was sore and my lungs were full, so nothing else mattered to me. Fuck Marcus. I couldn't wait to help Feelow set his ass up. I heard that nigga was fucking a cracker bitch now like a sista's pussy wasn't good enough anymore.

I needed a hit and Feelow was still asleep. I didn't want to wake him up, so I got up quietly as I could and walked to the table to fix me one up. I was still naked because Feelow wouldn't let me put on any clothes. He thought I would try to slip away on his ass, but the thought hadn't even crossed my mind, at least, not until the dope was gone.

***

I had been calling Feelow's phone for two days and still didn't get an answer. I threw my phone down on the bed and woke up the bitch that laid beside me. "What's wrong?" she asked as soon as her eyes opened.

I looked at her and felt disgusted so I said, "Bitch. You is what's wrong. Get yo' ass up and take care of this muthafuckin hard on I got."

She gave me a crazy look and said, "Nigga you ain't gonna be talking to me like that. You talk to yo' bitch like that, not me."

I grabbed her by her hair and pulled her to me and said angrily, "Ho, you don't know shit about my bitch so don't get yo' wig split up in this muthafucka."

She grabbed my wrists and said, "Ow Marcus, let me go. I'll do it. Just let me go."

I let the bitch go and said, "You know what? Fuck you. Bitch, I'm outta here." I put my pants on, picked up my shoes, and left the bitch behind.

I hadn't been home in a couple of days and I finally decided to show my face. I walked in and expected an argument but got something totally different. Krystal was in the kitchen cooking when she heard me enter. She asked, "You hungry?"

I responded, "Yeah. A nigga could use a little something. What you making?" If she wanted to play calm, I'd play that shit with her.

She answered, "Scrambled eggs, grits, sausage, and homemade buttermilk biscuits." My stomach growled loudly at the sound of it.

She fixed me a plate, sat it in front of me, and said, "Get your stomach full, baby." Her real white ass had me throwed off and made me feel like she was up to something, but I didn't think she was dumb enough to try me.

I asked suspiciously, "Yo, what's up with all this? Why you ain't questioning me and cussing me the fuck out? My ass ain't been home in two days and you acting all nonchalant and shit. What the fuck is up with that?"

She fixed her a plate and sat a glass of orange juice down beside mine and then she joined me at the table and said, "Well Marcus, I'm sure you put up with enough bullshit out in them streets. You shouldn't have to come home and deal with it here, too. Home should be your place of refuge from all that stress. Besides, if you had to stay gone for two days, I'm sure you had a good reason." She paused to take a bite of her food and then said, "My momma raised me very well up until her dying day. I either accept you as you are or I leave and since I'm feeling you and wanna be with you, I'm gonna take your flaws and all. I'm gonna be that bitch you can't ever replace. So, enjoy your breakfast."

Her answer threw me off balance, but it made me look at her differently. I gained a whole new respect for her after that. Bitches always wanted to question a nigga when he don't come home and the thought of not having to worry about that eased my mind. She was a real woman, my woman, and yet I couldn't keep my dick in my pants. Hell, a nigga needed variety in his life, but I'd kill her ass if she ever gave my pussy away. "I got to go out of town for a few days. You cool with that?" I asked.

She looked up at me with those eyes and answered, "Sure, I'll be here waiting for you. Just make sure you come back to me."

I nodded my head at her and said, "Nah Boo, pack a bag. Your white ass is going with me."

***

When I woke up, I felt like I had been hit by a semi-truck. I rubbed my morning hard and then remembered Keisha. I turned my head to look at her, but the space beside me was empty. I sat up real quick and then jumped out of the bed so I could locate her, but I knew in my gut that she was gone. I picked my pants up off the floor and checked my pockets. I noticed that some of my cash was missing but was thankful that she didn't take all of it. I went into the bathroom to make sure she wasn't there and didn't find her. I took a piss and then turned the water on in the sink, so I could wash my face and rinse my mouth. I grabbed a towel to dry my face off and walked back toward the door. I rushed over to her and gripped her neck with my hand and asked, "Bitch, where the fuck you been? Didn't I tell your ass not to leave?" The fear she held in her eyes didn't faze me, and I knew I wouldn't hesitate to break her neck.

She tried to explain through clenched teeth, "I went to get us some food. That's all." I looked down and on the floor beside her feet was McDonald's bags.

I let her go and said, "When I tell you not to do something, I mean that shit." I noticed that she had on my t-shirt and boxers with no shoes and felt kinda bad. I had locked her clothes in the back of my car to try to prevent her from leaving, but still, she managed to go.

"Nigga, I've been held up in here smoking this shit and fucking for two days and ain't ate a damn thing. My black ass is hungry, and I know you gotta be too." She bent down, picked up the bags of food up off the floor, and then walked up closer to me. She put a hand around my dick and said as she stroked it. "I know this pussy is good and all, but you ain't gonna get full just from eating it, daddy." She tiptoed and rose up enough to run her tongue over my bottom lip before, she pulled it into her mouth and sucked it. When she let it go she said, "You can suck on this clit for dessert, but for now, yo ass gotta eat some real food. I gotta keep you strong because I'm a lot to handle."

I reached an arm around her, pushed my free hand down in the boxers, and grabbed an ass cheek and then bent my head down for a kiss. I heard my stomach rumble while our tongues danced to a beat of their own. When I let her go, we shared a laugh? She walked over to the table and took out the food she had brought us and said, "I know good dick when I got it and you ain't gotta never worry about me going anywhere." I listened to what she said, but for some reason I smelled bullshit.

***

When I left the motel, I had no intention of going back, but I thought better of it and decided it would be best if I did. I needed to make Feelow trust me, so I could get deep up under him. I was shocked to learn about his beef with Marcus and wondered if Marcus even knew they had it. They had been partners for as long as I could remember, so something big had to have happened. I had heard about Marcus being held up with a cracker bitch and wondered if that was the cause, but then I remembered what I'd seen a few days earlier.

I had stood in shock as Feelow and another man walked up to the door of his crib. They asses seemed a little too friendly to me so my nosy ass decided to try to steal a peek. I walked around to the back of Feelow's place and saw that the window was slightly ajar. I bent the blinds apart, and that's when I saw Feelow standing in front of the other man as he stroked the stranger's dick. I was in shock at the scene I stumbled upon but decided that I would one day use the information to my advantage. I pulled out my phone and recorded the footage because that was the only way anybody would ever believe me.

Chapter Fifteen

The ride to Augusta was smooth without any hiccups. My mind was clear because I had left Trap over the crew. I knew that he would handle shit right while I was away. Next to Feelow, he was my most dependable soldier. I looked over to the white girl in my passenger seat and hoped that I'd made the right choice by bringing her with me. I'd already let her in on a lot of shit, and she'd had yet to fail me.

I pulled up to the warehouse that Temple had told me to meet him at and shut the engine off. "You ready?" I asked Krystal.

With a smile, she answered, "Baby, I stay ready. Let's go." She opened her door and I watched as she got out.

I said out loud to myself, *"Bold ass cracka."* It was as if she heard me because as soon as the words left my mouth she turned around.

I got out and followed behind her, but left my money in the ride. I would send Krystal back out to get it when everything was said and done. I banged on the door with the coded knock I was told to use and a big black ugly muthafucka answered. He didn't acknowledge me, but looked at Krystal like she was his next meal. I reached over, pinched one of her nipples, and said, "Bitch pretty as fuck ain't she? Too bad the bitch is mine and I don't like to share."

I was informed to show up unarmed, or he would have caught a slug about my bitch. I heard a voice in the background say, "Yo Skip, you gonna let 'em in, so we can handle this business or you just gonna-" His words were cut short because when he came to the door, he was taken aback by the presence of the white girl.

"You nigga. You ain't tell me your passenger was a white girl. What's up with that?" he stated while he looked Krystal up and down.

I started to speak, but Krystal held her hand up and spoke for me. "The only color that should matter here is the color of the money we came to spend. So, we gonna do business or should we take our money to another motherfucker?"

Temple stepped up closer to her and said, "You got a lot of mouth, white girl, but I like it." He then stepped to the side and allowed me and Krystal to walk in. There were hundreds of guns lined up on the table in front of us and as I admired them, Temple admired my bitch. I continued with my task and tried to ignore what went on behind my back. I didn't believe Krystal would do anything to disrespect. However, I needed this nigga, so I played along.

***

I ain't gonna lie, that nigga Temple was on point. I watched his eyes scan every piece of me and although, I knew not to ever cheat on Marcus, Temple's interest would come in handy one day. I knew Marcus fucked other bitches, but it wasn't enough for me to be disloyal. He would have to do way more than that to make me betray him.

***

"Aye yo, Temple. Can you step off my bitch long enough to handle this shit?" I asked while my trigger finger itched, even though I wasn't armed.

He took one final look at her and then walked over to where I was and said, "Nigga, if I stepped on her she wouldn't be your bitch anymore." I ignored his comment and placed my order.

I looked at Krystal and said it in a voice she knew that meant she would pay for her actions later on. "Go out and get the money."

She immediately walked out and when she did, Temple started in, "Nigga, you should let me show her what being with a brotha is all about." He grabbed his dick and continued, "Let me fill her up with something grown." Before I could respond, Krystal walked back inside and dropped the duffel bag at Temple's feet.

His boy Skip picked up the bag, counted the money, and then nodded his head to let Temple know it was good. "Bag up his shit so they can get the fuck outta here," Temple said as he stared me down. Skip did as his boss ordered and bagged up two Mac 12's, two AP 9s, four 380's, four glocks and two ten millimeter pistols. I knew that this would be the last time I'd do business with Temple, and told myself that one day I'd be back to take him out with one of the same guns he'd just sold me.

"Good business, man, but I don't think I'll need your services again."

I hung the bag over my shoulder and grabbed Krystal's hand to leave. When I did, Temple said to her, "Aye yo, white girl. When you ready to stop dealing with that little boy, let me know. I'll be right here."

She shook her head and said back to him, "Nah, he's man enough for me. I'm good." Deep down, Temple knew that one day she would return.

"I should go back up in there and kill that muthafucker," I stated angrily after I slammed my door. I turned to Krystal and grabbed her by the throat. "Bitch, don't ever think I won't kill yo' ass too. Don't you ever disrespect me." She batted her hands at me, but her strength would never match up to mine.

I finally let her go and she coughed until she got her breathing back and said, "Ain't that why you kept me, Marcus? So I could be entertainment for your connects? Huh, Marcus?" She rubbed her neck and continued, "You wouldn't know a real bitch if one slapped you in the face because deep inside, you flaw as fuck." What she said, hit a deep spot inside of my soul, and I wondered if her statement was really true. I had always been loyal and respectful to those I fucked with. At least that's what I thought. I brushed her comment to the side and hoped that one day those same words didn't bite me in the ass.

I had to drive the speed limit going back because I couldn't afford getting pulled over with that many guns on us. I had them hidden in a secret compartment that was built in the back seat, but still stayed alert. I looked over at Krystal who was still pouting, and my dick instantly got hard, so I reached over and rubbed on her thigh and asked, "You forgive me, baby?"

She turned her head, looked at me sideways, and said, "Fuck you, Marcus."

"Oh, yeah. That's what I want you to do. Fuck me. Come on, baby. Let a nigga feel on something wet," I said lustfully as I ran my fingers up to her breast and rubbed on a nipple through her t-shirt. When I did, it got hard instantly.

"Stop, Marcus. I ain't giving you no pussy," she said with a smile on her pretty face. I moved my hand off her breast and undid my pants. When I pulled my dick out, Krystal licked her lips and said, "Well, I guess I could use something to drink."

***

I heard a vehicle pull up outside and looked out the window. When I saw it was Feelow, I immediately got up and opened the door. I noticed that he wasn't alone, and who he had with him concerned me. We gave each other dap when he walked inside and Keisha looked at me sideways and asked, "What's up, Trap?"

I grabbed her fat ass and said, "This dick is what's up." She smiled and continued to follow Feelow inside.

I shut the door behind them and then went to the back room to get the money I owed for the five keys that Feelow had brought me days earlier. "Damn Trap, yo' ass be getting rid of that shit like it ain't nothing," Feelow said while Keisha stood beside him.

I said, "Yeah, ain't that what I'm paid to do?" I hope you brought me some re-up."

Feelow responded, "Nah, man. I'ma swing by and meet up with Marcus, so I can make that pick up and then I'll be back." As soon as he said it I knew something was off, but I continued to act normal, at least until I talked to Marcus.

"Yeah, I been calling that nigga, but it keeps going to voicemail. Tell him to reach out to me when he gets a chance," I said just to play along. I knew Marcus had went to Augusta and wouldn't be back until the next day, but Feelow's words made me realize that he didn't know anything about the trip. I knew from my last encounter with Feelow that something was amiss in the brotherhood, and this encounter made me see it was deeper than I ever could have imagined.

Feelow said, "Yeah, I'll let him know." He pulled Keisha close and kissed her, which confused me even more, and then said, "Me, him and Keisha gonna have a good time tonight. You're more than welcome to join."

"Nah, I'm good. I'm just gonna wait here for you to bring me that work back," I said. He picked up the bag full of money and turned to walk out. I followed him back to the door and before I shut it, I said, "Make sure Marcus gets my message."

***

As soon as Krystal wrapped her hand around my dick, my cell rang. I was going to ignore it but decided I should at least see who it was and when I saw Trap's number across the screen, I knew I had to answer. "What up, T. I hope this shits important 'cause I'm trying to get wet up right now," I said into the phone.

Trap responded, "Yo Marcus, tell ya bitch to let the dick go because you got more important things to worry about." I caught on to the seriousness of his voice, pulled Krystal off my dick, and asked, "What's up, man? Tell me what's going on."

His next words fucked me up. "Feelow just stopped by and picked up that gas money for you for those five gallons of gas you sent me. He said he was meeting up with you later." I hit the dashboard and caused Krystal to jump. Then Trap continued, "That ain't all, man. That nigga had Keisha with him and was kissing on her and shit like she was his bitch. He said all three of y'all 'pose to be getting it in tonight."

"Did you tell him I was out of town?" I asked.

Trap stated, "Hell, nah. I ain't no dumb ass nigga. I stood there and acted like I believed him and as soon as he left I called you."

"Aiight Trap, thanks for that information. I'm gonna go ahead and pull in tonight, so I can try to find out what's up with that nigga. Have the crew on standby just in case I need them." Then I hung up.

Krystal didn't ask any questions, but looked at me caringly and said, "It's all good, Boo. I'll take care of you later. Go handle your business."

My heart shattered into a million pieces when Trap told me about Feelow. I couldn't understand what had gotten into him, but I still didn't want to count him out just yet. The thought of him and Keisha crossed my mind and for him to be with her told me he was more off balance than I thought. Feelow couldn't stand Keisha so I had to figure this shit out, so I would know how to play into it. For him to fuck with her, he needed her for something, but my question was…For what?

Chapter Sixteen

"I called all of you here today because there may be some shit about to go down, on the same blocks you control," I said as I looked around the room to make sure I had everyone's attention. I then continued, "Some of those same niggas you work alongside are about to turn into your enemies unless you have the power to convince them to stay on your side."

Point Blank asked, "Man Ditto, what the fuck you talking 'bout? Quit drawing this shit out and speak straight to us."

"I'm talking about Marcus and his crew," I said sternly.

Trap cut in, "Man, we work beside them niggas and have been for a while. You sho' you ain't just paranoid or something."

"I won't take that as disrespect because I know I may have y'all confused right now but let me break this shit down." I took a deep breath and then continued, "Marcus no longer wants to report to me. He wants to venture out on his own and control his own territories, which would create competition."

Battie put in his two cents, "What's wrong with that, Ditto? You afraid the lil nigga gonna make more money than you?" Him and the others shared a laugh at the comment, but I wasn't up for jokes.

"You bitches find something funny?" I asked, and all laughing ceased. Him making more money than me is not a concern. My concern is him getting his product elsewhere and cutting me out, which is the same as cutting y'all out. I bet y'all niggas don't find that funny."

Montell said with his arms crossed over his chest, "Yeah and you already pay me pebbles, so I damn sure can't afford to take a loss."

"Nigga, I could make it where you gotta depend on a McDonald's check if yo' ass got a problem with what I pay you," I said and meant every single word.

The room erupted in loud shouts and chattering. I looked over at Stone and when he read the look in my eyes, he cocked his pistol and let off a shot. Pfft! The chair shattered into pieces from the impact of the bullet and caused everyone in there to get quiet. When I had their full attention back I continued, "Now if there is anyone in here who got a problem, speak that shit now so it can be handled." No one said a word back so I broke down what I needed them to do, "Point Blank, you the strongest nigga I got out there, so you go from spot to spot and make sure nothing seems off. Play it cool with Marcus' soldiers so they don't suspect anything." I then turned to Tray Pop and said, "I need you to continue on the Southside. If Micro and Corey act strange, don't ask questions. Blast them niggas. Paris, you and Montell keep an eye on Trap and Creep in the bottom. Those niggas won't hesitate to blast off if Marcus gives the order. And Tripp, stay on the North and keep dealing with Datsun and Black the same way you always have." I then looked to Battle. "You keep chillin with C-John and Blow. See if you can make 'em slip up and talk about it. I need to find out Marcus' plan and who he's switching to."

Everyone nodded their heads and agreed to the plans. I didn't think that any of my soldiers would abandon ship because they knew the consequences would be severe. However, I'm the one that taught Marcus everything and knew that he could very well use those same lessons against me.

***

No sooner than I hung up with Trap, my cell buzzed again, "Damn nigga, where the fuck you been?" I said into the receiver and waited for a response.

Feelow said, "Yo man, I ain't gonna lie. I was a little ashamed when you caught me on that secret I have and just wanted to lay low a few days, but I done switched back up and laid in some pussy for a couple of days. Shit was so good; I turned my phone off cause I ain't want nothin to interrupt it. Yeah baby, just like that. Mmmm… Mmmm."

"Hell nah, nigga. It sounds like you still laid up in it," I joked after hearing him moaning.

He said, "Man, this bitch can sho' suck a dick. Shit. Hold up bruh, I'm 'bout to shoot a load down this bitch tonsils. Shit. Yeah bitch, catch that shit. Swallow that nut. Mmm Hmm. Aiight, take a break while I finish talking to my boy."

"Man, if that bitch sucking dick like that then maybe I need to come where you at," I said.

Feelow responded, "Man, we can make that happen. Anyway, I called because I went to the bottom to pick up the gas money from Trap and bruh, I hate to be the bearer of bad news, but shit wasn't right when I counted it."

I snapped, "Nigga, what the fuck you telling me?"

"Dawg, shit was about eight short. I counted it three times by hand after the machine counted it, and it just didn't add up. What you want me to do?"

I knew it was a lie because Trap had been with me from day one and he never came up short, but I played into Feelow's words, "Nigga, you sho'? I ain't neva had an issue with Trap."

"Man, I'm telling you. I know I kept some personal shit from you, but my nigga, I wouldn't ever play with you like this. That shit was definitely off." I heard a female say something in the background and although, I knew it was Keisha, I didn't let on. I then heard Feelow say, "Let me see you play with that pussy while I finish talking to my boy. Yeah bitch, just like that. Damn nigga, you should see this bitch pulling on that clit like it's a dick. Damn."

I cut him off, "Fee, tell me where you at so I can meet up with you. Maybe even dig in some of that pussy you got there. Then we can figure out what to do next."

Feelow shut me down, "Nawl dawg, I'ma let this bitch ride this dick one mo' time, and then I'll meet you at the spot. We gonna have to schedule that ménage a trois for another time. This bitch claim she got somewhere to be, but I'll set it up. I'll meet you in an hour. Peace!"

With the dial tone in my ear, I sat there and thought about all the shit me and Feelow done been through together, and then I tried to figure out what had went wrong. I snapped out of it and decided that since I had an hour to kill, I might as well spend it in some pussy.

***

"Aiight Keisha baby, come sit on this dick one more time," I said while I piled some dope on the stem and melted it.

Keisha asked, "Can I hit it while I'm riding that fat dick?" I stroked my dick with one hand and held the pipe out to her with the other. She put it to her mouth and lit it and as soon as she exhaled, her pussy swallowed my nine inches.

"That's right Keisha, ride that dick. Ride this big muthafucka and think about how yo' nigga is about to put the city on lock. Yeah. Make this dick cum hard for daddy and I'm gonna bless you really well. Yeah, shit. Just like that," I said in deep pleasure while Keisha worked on my hardness and my mind worked on the story I was about to put down to Marcus. I knew that I was his most trusted man, and I planned to use that to my advantage. The streets were about to be mine, and anybody who stood in my way was going to get fucked in the ass.

***

Feelow thought he was smart, but he was just as dumb as the next nigga. I had been getting high for a while now, but still took good care of myself so no one ever caught on. His dumb ass thought he was turning me out, but it was actually the other way around. Especially since, I knew of his little secret.

Chapter Seventeen

"Yo man, nigga got me fucked up if he think I'ma be a fucking spy for his ass. I ain't keeping my eye on shit. Fuck that muthafucka," Paris said to Montell.

Montell nodded his head and responded, "That nigga don't pay me enough to watch what the next man does. Shiit, I say we go to Marcus and get down with his set."

With my hand on the steering wheel and my eyes on the road, I picked up my cell and dialed a number. "Yo, me and Montell on the way over to see you. It's time to implement that pact we discussed." I hung up and looked over at Montell and said, "We bout to light Ditto's ass up."

"Yo Creep, nigga give that pussy a break and come out here man!" I hollered through the door. I had grown tired of listening to Creep and Netta fuck like there was no tomorrow. I liked to fuck too, but my money came before bitches. I was fine with the occasional head job because I wanted to save my long stroking skills for when the right bitch came along. I wasn't trying to catch no diseases. The last bitch I fucked with gave me an STD after we had been together for years. I had given her everything, and all she gave me in return was syphilis. Now, I would rather stroke my shit myself or pay a trick a few dollars to suck me off.

I needed a bitch that I could fuck raw and possibly put some seeds in, but I wanted to get out of the game first because the game didn't play fair with black men. I didn't want to risk leaving behind a woman and children to move on without me, so I would continue to wait like I'd been doing. Creep, on the other hand, didn't mind running up in random hoes as long as he got his. Netta would be no different because when he was ready for some new pussy she would be history, but it was time to handle business so the pussy would have to wait until later.

***

I had my dick deep in the pussy, but my mind was deep in the game. I was anxious to look Feelow in his eyes just to see if he would lie to my face. There was no way he could convince me that Trap's money was short, although I knew he was about to try. Trap would cut himself short before he would fuck off with my money. However, I would play along with Feelow until I could figure out just what I wanted to do with him.

"Damn nigga, is you gonna fuck me or you gonna lay in it?" the bitch under me snapped. I looked at that ho like she was crazy and then pulled my dick out.

"Bitch, yo pussy so loose I ain't even realize I was in that muthafucka yet," I said back. Then I added, "Man, get the fuck up and get outta here. I got shit to do." She smacked her lips and hesitated, so I stood up and started putting my clothes on.

"Come on, Marcus. I ain't mean that shit. Come here and let me make it up to you," she begged, but my mind wasn't on the pussy anymore, so she was shit outta luck.

She laid back and started playing with herself hoping to lure me back in, but to no avail. "MMM Marcus, this pussy so wet. Come on and fuck me." I just shook my head and then walked out without saying anything.

I heard the room door open behind me while I walked to my car, then I heard the shouting, "Fuck you, motherfucker. Yo dick game is whack anyway. That little piece of meat couldn't please a damn baby, bitch!" I paid that ho no attention as I sped out of the parking lot and dialed Feelow's number.

He answered by the second ring this time, "Yo yo, my man. I'm on my way to the spot now. I'll see you there," Feelow said into the phone. I was happy to hear him sound like his normal self again and it made me almost feel bad for tripping on him.

I decided to call Trap and let him in on what was going on. "Holla at me yo," Trap said when he answered.

I didn't waste any time. "Aya, Trap. I'm just calling to let you know that I got word from Fee saying yo' pot was eight short so I'm..."

"Hell, no. Fuck that nigga. Marcus, you know better than that, shit. I'll kill that black bastard!" He hollered into the phone cutting me off mid-sentence.

When he was done with his ranting, I said, "Look, T. I know that nigga lying, but you gotta play along with my moves for now. At least until I figure out what's going on with him. Feelow acting strange and shit. That nigga is like my own flesh and blood, so his actions is fucking me up. I'm on my way to meet with him now. Just give me a minute to figure this shit out."

"Yeah aiight man, but if that muthafucka don't make shit right, I'ma smoke his ass, Boss Man," Trap said in a lower tone.

"Yo man, that's my brotha you talking 'bout, so eat that shit for now. If he's being disloyal, I'll handle him myself. I won't put that shit on anybody else. I'll call you later." Then I hung up.

***

I knew that other than me, Trap was Marcus' next in command, so in order to get the heat off of me, I would put it on him. There's no way that my brotha would believe that nigga over me, and if he did, he could kiss my black ass. The eight thousand dollars I took out of the money would be put up and every time I made a pickup I would add to my stash until I had enough to take to a new connect. I was going to sit Marcus down once and for all. That shit had been a long time coming and I was just the nigga to pull it off.

***

When I busted into the room all I saw was Netta's pussy looking back at me. "Yo man, shut that shit down. We got some serious shit going on and I need yo' ass on board," I said through Creep's moans.

He had his eyes closed, but opened them as soon as he heard my voice and said, "Man, just give me two more minutes. I'm about to bust in this bitch mouth."

I was sick of the bullshit so I walked over to the bed and snatched Netta up by her weave and said, "Bitch, take your ass home and check on your son. Nigga ain't gonna have no skin left on his dick if he keep fucking with your ass."

She looked at me through squinted eyes and said, "You acting like you mad cause it ain't your dick in my mouth."

I picked her clothes up off the floor, threw them at her hitting her in the face, and said, "Ho, you'd need a bigger mouth to suck on this dick. You betta ask yo' momma 'bout this muthafucka."

She jumped up off the bed with an attitude and looked at Creep for assistance. When she didn't get a reaction from him she said, "Fuck both of y'all niggas." Then she stormed out of the bedroom butt ass naked.

After a couple of minutes, she came back in and asked, "Creep, are you gonna take me home or what?" He got up off the bed and picked his pants up off the floor.

He dug in his pockets to pull out his knot and peeled off a five-dollar bill and then got up and put it in her hands and said, "Here, call a cab to take yo' ass home.

She looked at the crumpled money in her hand and said, "Nigga, this little money here ain't gonna get me nowhere, but up the street."

He looked back at her as he got dressed and stated, "Then I guess you better find you a dick to ride."

"Uh. You fucking piece of shit. Wait till I see Milo. I'ma put him on your ass for this shit," she said and then walked out slamming the door behind her. Little did she know, she'd be seeing Milo real soon.

***

I knew shit had to be serious for Trap to just walk in on me like that. I could see the look in his eyes when he pulled Netta off my dick. I asked, "Yo T, what the fuck going on man?" I sat down on the bed while he paced the floor in front of me, and then told me what went down.

"Yo, that nigga Feelow came by and picked up the gwap for them five and then called Marcus telling him it was eight short."

I stood up instantly and looked at Trap like he had spoken to me in a foreign language. "Nigga, quit fuckin playing with me and tell me what's really going on."

He stopped pacing, looked me dead in my eyes, and asked, "Do I look like my ass is running bullshit? Why the fuck would I play about something like that?"

I immediately pulled my gun from out of the drawer beside my bed and said, "Well, let's go smoke that nigga then. Bitch need to be taught a lesson on who to fuck with."

"Nah, man. Marcus said to chill and act normal. So, we gonna wait and see what happens. He on his way to meet up with that nigga now," Trap said in a calm voice.

"Wait. What the fuck you mean wait on Marcus? That nigga and Fee like brothas. He trusts that nigga more than anybody else. He shoulda listened to that nigga Ca$h who wrote Trust No Man. You got me fucked up if you think I'ma wait on his ass," I said angrily and started to walk out.

Trap grabbed my arm and said, "Nah, man. We gonna do what Marcus said. We move on his word. Nigga ain't neva led us wrong before."

My trigger finger itched, but I decided to listen to my boy. His mind had always been a little more level than mine because I wouldn't hesitate to bust a cap.

"Aiight, Dawg. I'ma chill. But, if Marcus' word don't get heard soon. We gonna move without him," I said and put a bullet in the chamber.

***

When I pulled up to the meeting spot, Feelow was already there. I made sure my burner was loaded and ready just in case he tried some shit. I hoped it wouldn't come to that shit, but if it did, I'd have to handle my business. If I got weak and spared Feelow the rest of the crew may have lost all respect for me and felt like they could try me too. Once I checked it, I put it down the waist of my pants and got out.

My skin crawled as I walked to the door, and before I could turn the knob, it opened. "What's up, bruh? I feel like we ain't seen each other in forever," he said as he held his hand up for some dap and then pulled me in for a brotherly hug.

"You got it, man," I said with a warm smile. He shut the door behind us and I walked over to the sofa we had set up along with a flat screen television to catch a game or two when we were held up there. Feelow sat in the chair opposite the sofa and as we faced each other, there was an uncomfortable silence. I decided to start the conversation since he acted like he was at a loss for words.

"Yo, man. What's this shit you telling me bout Trap?" I asked as I looked into his eyes, searching for some truth, but for some reason, I could no longer read him. I wondered if we had really drifted that far apart.

"Ah, man. I don't know what's going on with that nigga, but I counted that shit over and over, but still got the same results. Each time it was eight short. I ain't wanna go back and say nothing until I checked with you first though."

"Hmmm. That don't sound like Trap, dawg. That nigga always be on the mark," I said, defending the general of my squad. Trap was a real ass nigga and had been from day one. He didn't even have a steady woman because he said he didn't need or want anything to make him lose focus. He would get a trick to suck his dick once in a while, but never laid down with them hoes. He lived by his words, if you lay down with dogs, you are bound to catch fleas. He said when he got his money up and retired that was when he would find a shawty and chill and to this day, he has stuck to his word.

"Well, that nigga was off the mark on this money." He paused and then added, "You know Netta hungry ass been over there for days tricking off them niggas. Bitch might have stuck her hand in the pot without them knowing it."

I turned my focus to the game that was on the television screen and thought for a second before I responded, "Yeah, but I don't see them niggas being careless and leaving shit lying around like that for anybody to get in. Besides, Netta ain't that smart."

Feelow said with a half-smile, "Yo man, that dumb bitch ain't even checked on Lil Milo for days, so that ho had to be up to something. Bitch still think Milo coming home one day, but yet the stupid bitch can't even keep her panties on." He paused for a second and asked, "Dawg, when you gonna let her know about Milo?" I had thought about it ever since it happened, but still hadn't gotten around to it. I decided to stop by there on my way home and break the news to her. I'd make sure to drop her off some cash once in a while for Milo's seed since it was my fault he didn't have a daddy anymore.

"Aye, you want me to handle this shit?" I looked in his eyes and knew what he wanted me to say, but he would be disappointed.

"Nah, Fee. I got to go by that way anyway, so I'll drop by and see if I can find out what happened. I'll call if I need you," I said as I got up from the sofa and reached my hand out to give him some dap.

He got up, picked up the duffel bag from off the floor beside him, passed it to me, and then said, "Nigga, you know I got you whenever you call, right?"

"Yeah, Fee. Yeah. I already know you got me," I said as I looked up into his lying eyes, and then walked out.

Chapter Eighteen

It wasn't hard getting away from Ditto long enough to handle what I needed to handle. All I had to do was slip a pill in his drink and he was out for the next few hours. When I got that call from Paris, my heart sped up in excitement. It was the call I'd been waiting on, so I could finally be free. I saw Paris and Montell sitting on the park bench as soon as I pulled up. I strapped up, not because I didn't trust them, but because you just never know who would be watching.

"Yo pops, you good?" Paris asked as I looked into his eyes. The same eyes his mother had lured me in with until Ditto closed them forever. I had met Towanda when I first started in the game, but she turned me down every time I approached her. She said she didn't date drug dealers so when I got my money up I left the game alone and tried again.

"You still in the streets? Cause I don't want no street nigga," she asked, but I refused to walk away until she gave in.

I said, "Nah, I gave that shit up just so I could have you. Come on, give me a chance."

She looked at me suspiciously and asked, "So if you ain't selling dope what you do now?" I didn't want to tell her that I was a hired killer so I made up another story.

"Girl, I'm a security guard now."

Suspiciously, "Mmm…hmm…. A security guard? What place you guarding, Stanley?" Only Towanda could call me by my government and make it sound so sweet, everyone else called me Stone.

I answered her, "Damn Towanda, does it matter? I ain't on the streets selling that shit no more. That's all you need to worry about."

She tapped her foot on the concrete for a minute and then said the words that I had been waiting to hear, "Okay, Stanley. I'ma see what you about. But you better not break my heart." From that day on me and Towanda were inseparable. Six months into our relationship she said, "Stanley, we gonna have a baby."

"A baby. I'm gonna be a daddy? Hell, yeah!" I said excitedly and was even happier when months later she gave birth to my son Stanley James Parrish Jr.

I wanted my son to have it all so against Towanda's pleading I jumped back into the dope game, however, I never brought anything back to where we laid our heads. Things were going good for the first couple of years until one day I got popped and was sent up the road. Them crackers gave me seven years, but that shit felt like a life sentence. It was hard to be away from my woman and my seed, but there wasn't shit I could do about it nor was there shit I could do for my family.

Towanda held me down for as long as she could, but the time got the best of her. It was hard out there, with her being a single mother with no money coming in, so she did what she had to do. She packed up Little Stanley and took him to her grandmother's because she could barely feed herself and didn't want him to suffer too. She soon started dating again because her lonely heart needed soothing, and her lonely body needed sexual healing. That was when she met Dittrick also known as Ditto.

Ditto was fresh in the game when he came across little Towanda, and after he wined and dined her for a couple of months, his true colors showed. He began to beat on her and also fucked other bitches while he made her sit in a chair beside the bed and watch. He would make her get undressed beforehand and tell her to play with her own pussy while he pushed his dick up in another one. Soon after he met the woman he would ultimately marry, and spent less and less time with Towanda who, although he treated like shit, was hooked and didn't want to let him go.

Towanda had enough, followed him and his new woman home one night, and approached them. "Nigga, get rid of that bitch, or I will," she stated angrily as she held a gun in his face.

He looked at her crazy and then knocked the gun out of her hand and said, "Bitch, you got some nerve. Who the fuck you think you talking to?" He then turned to his woman and said, "Go in the house. I don't want you to witness this." She immediately did as she was told and then Ditto grabbed Towanda by the hair and drugged her to the back of his car. He pushed her in the trunk and closed it. His strength outweighed hers, so she couldn't even fight him off. Ditto took Towanda to his warehouse and did all kinds of gruesome things to her. He fucked her in every hole she had with foreign objects and then beat her until she was unrecognizable all while she begged for her life. Then finally, with only eternal darkness left in her gaze he put twelve bullets into her body and walked out.

When I got out of prison after doing seven years, I'd heard about what happened and formed a plan. I left my ten-year-old son at the place he'd been while I did my bid and got a job as Ditto's right hand and enforcer. I wanted the timing to be perfect and then together me and Paris would get our payback. Ten years later, I was still working for Ditto and when Paris called about that pact we'd made I was good and ready. Ditto was so caught up in his own world that he never noticed the almost identical resemblance that me and Paris had, but one day soon, we would make his ass see double.

"Yeah son, I'm straight. How you been holding up out there?" I asked as I hugged my son and gave Montell some dap. Paris and Montell were thick as thieves and had been best friends since their diaper days. They knew Montell could be trusted. Montell had known that they were father and son, but never said a word to anyone. While Paris and I discussed our mission, Montell kept watch to make sure no unwanted guests popped up.

"Yo Pops, my dick gets hard every time I think about smoking that muthafucka," Paris said.

I shook my head and looked my mirror image in the eyes and said, "We got this, son. We going to make that nigga pay for that foul ass shit he did to yo' momma, but when it happens, we can't miss."

"Aye, we going to join forces with some of Marcus' crew and push that nigga out. The whole time his ugly ass was speaking at that meeting, my blood was boiling," Paris commented angrily.

"Well, you know I gotta keep playing my part until we can infiltrate his position. You get with Marcus and his squad and let me know the next move. Don't move too fast, though. Impatience could get you killed," I said and then I got lost in my thoughts for a second and continued, "Aiight son, this is what we need to do..."

I decided to wait before going to see Trap and Creep in the bottom but stopped by Netta's on my way home to Krystal. As soon as

I pulled up, she opened the door like she was expecting me. I walked right in when I got to the door and when I passed by her, she asked, “Did you come to finish what you started?”

I didn’t answer her, but instead went and sat on the couch and asked, “Where Lil Milo at?” She slammed the door and sucked her teeth before she walked over to where I sat.

When she got in front of me she pulled the t-shirt that she had on from over her head and then sat on the opposite end of the couch and said, “Don’t worry about him. He good. But, this pussy ain’t.” She spread her legs and opened her pussy as she pulled a nipple.

I shook my head while my dick rose and asked, “You ain’t get enough dick from Creep ass while you was over there?”

She looked at me seductively and answered, “It don’t matter how much dick, none of them stop me from wanting yours. So, what’s up?”

I shrugged my shoulders and said, “Well, bend that ass over then.”

Netta turned around and leaned over the arm of the couch while I undid my pants. I knew I didn’t have to worry about Milo walking in this time and disturbing the groove because he was now walking around the pits of hell. As soon as I put my dick to Netta’s wet hole my cell rang. “Shit,” I said out loud.

Netta turned her head to look at me and said, “Don’t answer that. Come on Marcus, give me the dick.” I almost listened to her, but decided I needed to at least see who it was and when I saw B-Line’s number, I answered.

“Yo, man, I been waiting on your call. What’s good?” I sat back down on the couch and Netta got up and stood in front of me. She pulled my pants down to my ankles and then swallowed my dick.

B-Line said, “Aye, I’m ready for you to make a trip this way. If you need more time I understand, but I got anotha nigga on standby if you can’t step up to the plate right now.” I motioned for Netta to turn around and bend over the table and as I talked to B-Line, I slid my dick up inside her.

"Hell, yeah. I'm ready, B. I'll pull up this Friday and stay the weekend if that's cool with you," I said as Netta's loud cries of pleasure damn near drowned out my words.

"Sounds like you already pulling up." B-Line laughed. "Call me as soon as you get in town. I'll be waiting." Then he hung up.

I hit end on my phone, tossed it on the couch, and fucked Netta a new pussy hole and right when I pulled out and came all over her back, I said, "Oh yeah, I forgot to tell you that Milo ain't neva comin' home."

She turned around like the matrix and asked, "What the fuck you mean Milo ain't comin' home?"

I said in a sorrow filled voice. "They found that nigga's body slumped in the back of a garbage truck. I'm sorry, Netta." And I meant it.

Her tears formed immediately as she spoke to me through broken words, "Damn, Marcus. I know I do some fucked up shit, but I loved that nigga. What are me and Lil Milo gon' do now? Besides my grandma he was all I had." I felt even worse for pulling the trigger that ended Milo's life, but what was done was done and I couldn't take it back.

I said, "Yo Netta, I'ma make sure that you and Lil Milo got what y'all need. That was my boy."

She looked at me crazy and asked, "Do you know who did it, Marcus?"

I lied to her with a straight face, "Nah, but I put the word out, and as soon as I find out who did it I'ma smoke they ass."

I pulled my pants up, got a knot out of my pocket, handed it to Netta, and said, "Take this for now. I'll drop something else off soon. It's the least I can do." Then I walked out of her house and left her with a freshly fucked pussy and a broken heart. I would check on her again soon, but my next visit wouldn't turn out like I expected.

***

I decided to go back down to the bottom, although Marcus said he would handle it. He had gotten soft, so I didn't expect him to handle shit. When I pulled up, Trap and Creep were sitting on the front porch as if they were expecting my arrival. Before I could even get out of the car, Creep walked up on me. "Nigga, what the fuck you talkin' bout us being short on our shit?" he asked while he put a hand on his burner.

"Yo, man. Chill," I said as I started to shut my door, but Creep yanked it back open and said, "Nigga get out and explain this shit to us to where we can understand it." Trap held the front door open and waited for Creep to escort me to it. I didn't even have a chance to grab my gun, so I had to be careful how I answered to them or I could very well lose my life. "Man, go the fuck in and sit the fuck down and if you make any sudden moves I'ma blast that ass," Creep said as he held the gun to my head.

I started talking as soon as I sat down. "Yo, I think Netta got y'all ass while she over here and ….."

Creep cut me off, "Bitch, Netta wasn't off my dick long enough to get her hands on anything, so you gotta come better than that." Trap stayed quiet as he sat in a chair across from me. He was the levelheaded one and I knew that because of the lie I told on him it would be hard to convince him of anything, but I had to try.

"Trap man, look I counted that shit three times and each time it was off. I know y'all shit always be straight, so it had to be that bitch. Man, I'm telling you Netta got y'all ass." He still didn't say anything so I looked up at Creep and said, "Nigga, maybe she got you when you went to sleep. I know you wasn't digging in that hole twenty-four straight, right?"

I could see the confusion in Creep's eyes as he thought about what I said and then responded, "Yeah, I took a couple of naps, but I don't believe that bitch is smart enough to pull that shit off."

"Think about it. That nigga Milo gone and ain't never coming back. He ain't never coming back. She ain't got no other way to take care of herself. Bitch gotta do something to feed her and Milo's lil bastard," I said convincing. Then added, "You should go check that bitch and see if she guilty and then rock that ho to sleep."

“Yeah, I think I will head over there and check it out, but yo ass going with me,” Creep said.

“Man, I got other shit to handle, so I’ma have a pass on that,” I said and got up to leave.

Creep put the gun back to my head and said, “Nah nigga, you riding because one of you muthafuckas gon’ come up with that bread or I’ma turn yo’ ass into sandwich meat.”

Trap hurriedly stood and placed a hand on Creep’s trigger arm and said, “Creep dawg, let shit go. We’ll square up with Boss Man and take care of Netta’s ass later.”

“Hell, no. Fuck this Muthafucka. Somebody gon’ answer for that shit because I know damn well that shit was straight,” Creep spat.

Trap said again in a calmer voice, “Let that shit go, Creep. We’ll handle that bitch next time she steps to our door. But, right now, we gon’ take it as a loss.”

I let out a sigh of relief when Creep finally listened and lowered the gun. Then I said, “When Marcus calls and tell me y’all straight I’ll be back to drop off the next bag, but I suggest you keep your dick outta the dirt, so you don’t gotta worry about being buried.” Then I walked out and slammed the door behind me.

I looked at Trap like he had lost his mind and asked, “Man, what the fuck wrong with you? That nigga ‘pose to be on the floor leaking right now. Got Marcus thinking we done fucked him on his money.”

Trap walked over to the window and looked out of it as if he were making sure Feelow was gone before he spoke. “We gon’ play this shit out like Marcus said. Don’t worry, Feelow’s gon’ get what he’s owed from us, but it ain’t gonna be in cash.”

I said to him in an agitated voice, “Marcus look at that nigga like his brotha. E gon’ let him get away with that shit and we gon be the ones getting fucked. That’s his man.”

“Yo, Creep. Just trust me on this. Marcus knows he’s lying. When we signed on with Marcus we pledged our loyalty and that’s what he gon’ keep givin. So, chill and let Marcus take care of that nigga. He brought Fee into this so let him take Fee out.”

I wasn't happy with what Trap said, but I had always listened to him and that time would be no different. I hoped his ass was right or we'd both be laid out on the concrete.

***

I heard the beating on the door and jumped out of the shower to go answer it. "Damn, I'm coming. Hold the fuck on. I'm coming, shit!" I said out loud as I tightened the bathrobe around my waist and opened the door. As soon as I did, his hands encircled my throat and cut off the screams I held inside. I tried my best to fend him off, but I had no strength inside of me. At that time, I was thankful that Lil Milo was still at my grandmother's because I didn't want him to witness this. I thought about Milo and wished that he were there because he never would have allowed that to happen. Although, I was a sinner, I sent prayers to GOD above to save me from this man's wrath. What I'd done to make him come at me like this was a mystery. Slowly, I felt my eyes get heavy and arms got weak. The fight in me was gone, and I looked him in his eyes one last time. As soon as he told me who killed Milo, the room went dark.

Chapter Nineteen

I heard him pull up but didn't even wait for him to put his key in the lock. I opened the door and went against everything my momma taught me. "Where the fuck you been, Marcus?!" I screamed at him, but he just pushed me aside like I was nothing, but a rag doll. I slammed the door and followed behind him because I wanted answers and wouldn't stop until I got them.

"I asked you a fucking question, Marcus. You disrespectful bastard," I spewed. He looked at me through his black heartless eyes and then walked up on me. He pinned me against the wall with his hand on my throat. His face was so close to mine that a piece of paper wouldn't have slid through it in between.

He said through clenched teeth, "Bitch, you got some nerve to question me in my shit. I don't owe you an explanation for anything, so you better check that shit."

When he let me go from his grasp, I went in, "Fuck you and whatever bitch you been in. I'm fucking leaving."

I turned to leave the room, but before I could even make it out the door, he grabbed my arm and pulled me back. "Bitch, why you worried about where my dick been at? Huh? That's what you want?" he hollered out and then threw me on the floor. "You want some of this dick. That's what your white ass cryin' about. Come on then. Let me give you some of this dick, so you'll shut your fucking mouth," he said angrily and then pulled out his dick and stroked it.

I sat up and said, "Fuck you, I don't want that shit. It's probably covered with next bitch pussy juice anyway."

He continued to stroke it and said, "Put it in ya mouth and see. Come on. Taste this big muthafucka." I looked up at him and then at the long, smooth tool he held in his hand and smiled. I had only sucked on it once, so I still wasn't that good, but I gave in and wrapped my lips around it anyway.

"That's right, baby. Yeah, just like that. You feel better now?" he asked as I took in all of him and moaned, "MMM HMM."

He stopped me mid suck and said, "Take them threads off and let a nigga get inside. I didn't even hesitate and less than a minute later he was deep inside of me as he talked shit, "Don't ever question me like that again. You hear me? Shit, this pussy good and wet."

Then I said in pleasure, "I won't, Marcus. Oh, my GOD you feel so good. I won't do it again. Yes."

After he fucked me real good and put me in my place he got up and said, "We got a trip to make, so get yourself together and pack up our shit. I'm going to take a shower." Then the heartless muthafucka left the room.

***

I don't know where that white bitch got off questioning me, especially after she said she would never do that. However, her attitude wasn't nothing that some dick couldn't take care of. All a nigga had to do was stuff some dick in a bitch, and it would set them back straight. I hopped in the shower and a minute later, Krystal came and hopped in with me. She took the washcloths off my body and caused my manhood to rise back up. I kissed her and said, "Turn around and bend over. I got a special treat for you." She smiled and then did as I said without comment. I kneeled down and licked from the top of her crack to the bottom, and then stood back up and slid inside of her.

When we were done, Krystal finished packing us some bags while I called Trap. "Boss Man, what's good?" he asked after answering on the first ring.

I said, "Aye, Trap. I gotta go outta town again, so I need you to hold it down for me. We gon' set some shit up when I get back."

"Yeah, well what you want me and Creep to do while you gone? That nigga Fee came by and said he wasn't moving shit with us until he got the call from you. Creep almost capped his ass, man. I had to stop him," Trap said.

"I'll call him before I pull out, but whatever you do, don't let him know I'm outta town. I plan on dealing with Fee real soon, so tell Creep to fall back. I gotta handle that on my own," I said disappointingly.

"Aiight man, bet. Let me know when you pull back in," Trap said. Then added, "And, yo. We ain't giving no more bread to that nigga. That shit going straight to you."

"Bet that, man. I'ma call Fee now, so he can set y'all straight. I'll holla when I get back," I said and then hung up and made my next call.

"What's up, my brotha?" Feelow asked when he answered. Him sounding like his old self had me confused and fucked up in the head, but I'd never let him know that.

I said, "Yo Fee, I need you to go ahead and fix up Trap and Creep. They squared up so shit is all good. I got some shit to handle, so I'll get up with you later."

"Yeah. I got you bro, but them niggas better come right this time or we gon' have to make an example out of 'em," Fee said in an agitated voice.

"Aiight, I hear ya. I'll holla," I said and hung up before he could say anything else. I was on another mission and wasn't up to listening to his bullshit. I'd deal with Feelow when the time was right because I had other shit to deal with first.

***

When I opened my eyes, the room spun around me and caused me to close them again. After a couple of minutes, I opened them back up and tried my best to focus on my surroundings. My heart sped up as my mind thought the worst and then once I realized I was at home, I breathed a sigh of relief. "Damn, I must have really been tired," I said to myself and got up out of the chair I had apparently passed out in.

I stumbled through the house looking for Stone, but he was nowhere to be found. Something was definitely off because Stone never left my side. My paranoia kicked in and made me think that something had happened to him. Right when I picked up my phone to dial his number, the entire room went black.

***

I watched Feelow as he pulled the black duffel bag out of his trunk and then looked around. He seemed paranoid as if he felt someone watching him. I said to myself, "Fuck it," and shrugged my shoulders. As I started to turn around, another vehicle caught my eye. I paid attention to the scene that unfolded before me because although, I had only been out of prison a little over a week, I knew almost everyone who came and went through my hood. If I didn't know them, I had at least heard their story because almost all of them were the same.

I heard my sister call my name from the front of the apartment but ignored her because I knew something was off about what was taking place. I kept my eyes glued to the parking lot, watched as Echo got out of his ride, and looked around the same way that Feelow had just done. He then followed the same path that Feelow had just taken to his front door.

Echo was and up and comer in the game when I had been sent away. He was the topic of many prison conversations because his status in the streets rose quickly. I'd heard he moved to Brooklyn and set up shop there. I'd also heard that he had a strong team behind him. His lieutenant was a female stud called Swag T, and they said that she was a force to be reckoned with. Echo, Swag T, and Echo's hitman Toe Tag were said to be looking for new territory to run in. So my question was, why was he with Feelow?

I had known Marcus my whole life, and I knew that him and Echo had a past beef in the streets way before Marcus grew his team. Echo relocated to Brooklyn, where he took over the Brownsville and Crown Heights areas. It was said that Swag T seduced a girl named Brandy who belonged to a nigga they called the King of Brooklyn or better known as Savage. Brandy suddenly became paranoid about her and Swag T's affair and told her that they could no longer get down, but Brandy was an asset to Echo's team because they wanted her to get to Savage. Swag tried, but failed to lure Brandy back in, so she put Toe Tag on the mission.

Toe Tag kidnapped Brandy while she was out shopping one day hoping to get Savage to come look for her. They made her call Savage to come rescue her. He laughed and said, "Nah, bitch. I'm good. I'll just replace you with another one." Then he hung up on her. Brandy begged and pleaded with Swag T to let her go, to no avail. Echo ordered Toe Tag to kill her a week later and then dumped her body in Savage's front yard.

When her murder didn't make Savage budge, Echo decided to try something else to bring Savage out. He had brought his sister a house out in Manhattan, so she would be away from him and all his enemies. She was all he had left and somehow Echo learned of her whereabouts. Echo, Swag T, and Toe Tag watched her for three days and then Swag made her call Savage. When he found out his sister was in harm's way, he came out of his hiding spot.

However, Echo was an impatient man. Toe Tag sat in her living room and waited for Savage to show up, but he was two minutes too late. When he finally showed up, his sister's brains were splattered all over her living room. With Savage on his knees, crying over the death of his only love on earth, Toe Tag walked up on him and put forty-five bullets into his body. Echo expected a war from Savage's side, but no one mourned his death or seeked revenge on his killer. Instead, they joined forces with Swag T and the rest was history.

After I watched Echo follow Feelow to his apartment, I walked away from the window and went to see what my sister wanted. "Damn. Nigga, why you ain't answer me when I hollered for your ass?" TyKita asked with an attitude.

I said, "Girl, you ain't want shit. Damn, can a nigga jack his shit without having to hear yo' damn mouth."

"Fuck you. It ain't my fault your ass ain't got no pussy since you been out. Shit. You need to go find something to fuck, so yo' ass can chill the hell out," she said and then reached in her purse and pulled out some money and added, "I need you to go pick me up some cigarettes. Shit, you might as well make yourself useful." I looked at her sideways, then snatched the money out of her hand, and took off for the door as TyKita hollered, "And look for a damn job while you out." I slammed the door behind me and as soon as I made it to the bottom of the steps, I saw Echo come back out.

***

Me and Marcus grew up around the corner from Echo and because a chic that Echo liked wanted Marcus instead, Echo had him jumped. The sad thing was that Marcus didn't even want the girl, so he got jumped on for nothing. Ever since then, Echo has hated Marcus and I used that to my advantage. I swore that I'd rather die than to ever betray my friend, but I was ready to play a bigger part in the game and I knew that I'd never be able to as long as I worked under Marcus.

I laid out the ten kilos Echo fronted me and felt my stomach turn in knots. I was gonna spend the next few hours repacking the kilos and cooking some up for my personal use. I would put the powder in the blender and cut the cocaine with aspirin and borax so that I could make it go further. I decided I'd do me a hit and then start on my mission. My mouth watered when I put a big rock on my stem and when I put it to my lips and lit it. I closed my eyes in pleasure. My dick rose immediately and as I blew the smoke from my lungs, my doorbell rang.

***

I couldn't move my arms and panicked before I realized that I was tied up. I lifted my head and looked around through blurred vision. I shivered from the coldness and then realized that I was completely naked. When my vision cleared, I noticed that I was in my warehouse, but how I got there was a mystery. Only my squad knew about this place unless someone had ratted me out. My first thought was Marcus. I had done everything for that lil nigga and this was how he repaid me. I wondered how long he would leave me like this. I decided that when he appeared I would agree to whatever he wanted until he untied me, and then I'd rip his heart out of his chest.

How could Marcus have gotten to me? I tried to remember being taken, but nothing came to me. My head bobbed up and down as I hollered, "Marcus, untie me you muthafucka! Show your face you fucking coward!" The chills stopped and sweat formed on my brow. I heard footsteps in the distance as they echoed off the floors. My breath quickened and my eyes focused on the figure that appeared before me, and once I saw who it was I breathed a sigh of relief.

***

The ride to Baltimore was relaxed and pleasant. Krystal was asleep in the passenger seat as I thought about the move I was making. When I first started with Ditto I hadn't planned to stay in the game this long, but now that I was this far in I couldn't see myself doing anything else. I knew that what I was about to do was going to start chaos in the streets, but I was already prepared for whatever Ditto brought my way. I wasn't scared of his ass. He either backed down or got knocked down. It was his choice, but one he didn't have long to make.

I pulled into the driveway of B-Line's house and was impressed. This was how I wanted to live one day, and now knew that I had made the right decision. "Aye, Krys. We here," I said to Krystal and nudged her awake. She opened her eyes and looked as if she had never been asleep. She had no clue what I had in store for her, but after this meeting, she would find out.

"Damn, I been asleep that long?" she stated as she unhooked her seatbelt and then added, "I guess if I would go to sleep at night instead of staying up waiting for your ass I wouldn't be so tired."

I grabbed her by the wrist and said through clenched teeth, "Keep talking shit, and you'll be waiting on somebody to come identify you."

She snatched her wrist out of my hand and said, "Yeah. Well, I'd probably be better off."

She opened her door, got out, and then went to the back door to open it and retrieve her bag. When she slammed it closed, she looked at me and shook her head as if she were disappointed. I got out and met her at the front of the ride and right before I started to slap her white ass, another voice spoke up.

***

I saw his hand go up like he was about to put a mark on the female he had brought with him, but it wouldn't happen in my presence. "We don't do that around these parts," I said as I looked at him with death in my eyes. I had watched my momma get beat on all of my life by my stepdad and it had done something to me. I tried to defend my momma one night, but he punched me so hard it knocked me out and by the time I woke up, my momma was dead. I swore that I'd never let that happen to another woman in my presence even if she was a stranger.

"Nah, B, it ain't even like that. What's up, yo?" Marcus said as he tried to play it off.

I looked at the female he had with him and was stuck for a minute and then asked, "How you doing, little lady? I'm Brandon. You can go on inside and make yourself comfortable while me and ya man here talk some business." She smiled and melted a piece of me. I knew this was going to cause a problem, but I'd never run into one I couldn't solve.

***

"Stone, nigga where the fuck you been at? How the fuck you let shit like this happen to me?" I asked angrily as Stone walked closer to me, "Nigga, hurry up and untie me." He suddenly stopped and stood there with a look in his eyes I'd never seen before. I'd never been afraid of Stone before he had always protected me, but at the moment, the fear in me rose. Something wasn't right about his demeanor. "Yo man, why you just standing there? What's up, nigga? Untie this shit, man," I stated in a more aggressive voice right before another figure appeared.

I looked at Stone in a confused manner when Paris appeared and stood beside him. "Man, what the fucks going on? Paris, why yo' ass ain't out there on my blocks?" I asked in a broken voice.

"Nah, man. Those ain't your blocks anymore. Damn dawg, you mean to tell me you ain't get the memo?" Paris said and then another figured appeared from the shadows and said, "Here ya go, man. This the meanest one I ever been around. This bitch is a beast." Montell then passed the leash to Paris.

My heart speeded up as I panicked even more. "Yo, Stone. Untie me so we can handle these lil niggas," I said nervously. Stone said nothing as he walked closer to me and then got behind me. "Stone, what's going on? Why you ain't untying me?" I asked after I realized he made no effort to free me.

He said from behind me, "Montell, thanks man, but you can go now. This is something that me and my son have to handle."

"Your son? What the fuck you talking about, Stone?" I asked and then looked to Paris and asked again, "Paris, what the fuck is he talking about?"

Stone then told me his story, "Well Marcus, a long time ago I met the love of my life. She was my everything and I worshipped the ground she walked on." He paused and sniffed as if he was on the verge of crying and then he continued, "Well, about six months into our relationship, she told me she was pregnant. God Ditto, that made me the happiest man in the world, and when she gave birth to my son I fell even more in love with her." He came around, pulled a chair up in front of me, and sat down.

I asked him, "Yo man, what the fuck that shit got to do with me?"

"Yo D, just shut the fuck up and listen to what I got to say potna," he said with a devious laugh and continued, "You see, when my son, Stanley James Parrish Jr was born, I wanted to give him the best of everything, so I jumped back in the dope game going against what his momma asked of me. I rode out for a few years, but when Little Stanley was three, I got popped and was sent away, leaving Paris here, and his momma behind."

"Nigga, what? Paris is yo' son? What the fuck?" I asked as I jerked in the chair trying to get my hands out of the restraints they were in. The pitbull stood and growled, but when Stone turned his head and looked at the dog, she sat back down and then Stone continued with his story. "Ya see Ditto, while I was away Paris momma took him to stay with her grandmother because she was having a hard time by herself and there wasn't shit I could do from behind the fence. She got lonely and looked for someone else to fill that void while I was gone. It broke my heart, but I couldn't fulfill those desires for her, so I had to let her go so she could do what she needed to do to be happy." I watched as tears formed in his eyes, and then he added, "She finally met someone, but that nigga treated her like shit. He cheated on her all the time. He ended up cutting her off for another bitch and when she confronted him, he beat her until her eyes swelled shut and then he filled her body with heat-"

I interrupted him and said, "Yo man, I'm sorry to hear that, but I still don't understand why the fuck you telling me this. Why you got me here like this?"

Stone stood from the chair and said, "Oh, Dettrick. I'm about to get to that. You see, I vowed to get the nigga that took my heart and soul from me. My son had to grow up without his momma and I could never imagine anyone replacing her. But, now, the time has come for revenge and nigga you gon pay for what you did."

"Man, what the fuck you mean. I ain't did shit. You got your information wrong. Stone man, chill cause I don't know what the fuck you talking about. Cut me loose, my nigga. We can find that muthafucka who did it together." I pleaded, but my pleas went unheard.

Stone nodded his head at Paris who then walked closer to me with the pitbull. I could see the hunger in the dog's eyes as drool slid off her tongue and dripped onto the floor below. "Man, come on. I don't know what the fuck you talkin bout. You got the wrong person," I pleaded one more time.

Stone looked me in the eyes and bent down to pet the dog and when he said, "Meet my bitch, Towanda," I pissed all over myself.

Chapter Twenty

I opened the door, saw Tyckori looking me in the eyes, and asked, "What up, Tyck? A nigga ain't even know you was out. Damn man, long time, no see." He held his hand out and when I shook it, I pulled him for a hug.

He pulled back from me and said, "Yeah Fee, it's good to see you too. I got out a little over a week ago, but I just been trying to get myself together. What's good with you?"

I opened the door further, so he could come inside and then he asked, "Was that Echo I just seen leaving?"

I said, "Yeah. That was that nigga. We was just handling a little business. As a matter of fact, come on into the kitchen."

When we walked in the kitchen, he saw all the cocaine on the table and whistled. I said, "I'm 'bout to blow up, my nigga. I'm trying to build me up a team and since you just getting out maybe I could help you get on your feet." I walked up closer to him and rubbed on his dick just to test the waters. He just finished a six-year bid so I knew he couldn't have went that long without a nut. He pushed my hand away forcefully and asked, "Yo Fee, what the fuck up with that?"

"Man, I don't mean no disrespect. I just thought since, well you know," I said and before I could finish my sentence, he interrupted.

"What? Since I was around nothing, but niggas for six years. That's what you was about to say? Nigga, I ain't even knew you swung like that," Tyck stated as he looked down at my hard dick.

"Man, I'm sorry, alright. I like women too, but men turn me on more. I like the feel of it sometimes, but let's keep that shit between us. Aiight?" I said hoping he would agree.

"Yeah. Aiight. It'll be our little secret," he said and then unzipped his pants.

"What's the matter, D? You don't like Towanda? That's funny 'cause you didn't mind my other bitch Towanda being on your dick," Stone said as Paris stood to the side and laughed. I was scared as a muthafucka and pleaded for my life.

"Yo, Stone. What the fuck you talking bout, man? I ain't understanding what you talking bout. We 'pose to be boys so let's work this shit out, man. Come on and untie me."

"Yeah, D. I'm sure Towanda begged for her life too, but yo' ass ain't spare her, so I'm not sparing you," Stone said with a look of heartbreak in his eyes. Then he continued, "She was the love of my life, D. I ain't neva loved another woman since. My heart won't let me. Muthafucka, you took her from me and our son. You did that shit and now, we gon' make you pay for it."

My heart sped up even faster when he unhooked the leash that was around the dog's neck. I cried out, "Man, I ain't know. Why you just now telling me that shit? I ain't mean to kill her, man. Shit just got outta hand. Come on, man. Give me a chance to explain."

Paris finally spoke, "Nigga, my momma ain't neva hurt nobody. She just wanted you to do right by her, but you treated her like shit you bastard. You didn't have to kill her. Bitch, I needed my momma, but you only gave a fuck about yo'self and since she ain't here to pay you back, we gon' get justice for her." He bent down beside the dog and whispered something in her ear right before she attacked.

***

"What you do with your bitch on your time ain't my business, but while you here, you gon' treat her like the queen of the world. Do I make myself clear?" I said as I looked Marcus in his eyes.

"Yeah, B. My bad, nigga. I can respect that," Marcus said as he held his hand out for some dap.

When I turned around, his girl was standing behind me and as soon as I looked in her eyes, I knew that me and Marcus wouldn't be doing business for long and she would be the reason why. I said, "Come on, let's go in and talk some business."

***

Being locked up at such a young age, and before I had a chance to discover the feeling of a female made me vulnerable to the men I would encounter. My first year in, I made a bet on a football game and lost. The victor wanted my innocence as payment, and once he turned me out, there was no going back. Finding out that Feelow got down too put me at ease. However, I would give Feelow what he liked just until I could find out what was going on.

For him to be getting work from Echo meant that someone was trying to cut Marcus out, and I wasn't about to let that happen if I could help it. Everyone in the dope game wanted to outshine someone else, and they would do whatever needed to be done to do just that.

"Damn Fee, you sho' know how to make a nigga feel good," I said as I pulled my pants back up. Fee put on his boxers and walked back into the kitchen, where I followed.

"Man, you can get it whenever you want it, as a matter of fact, I could use some company around here and a right-hand man to help me start this shit up. You down?" Fee asked.

I didn't even hesitate with my answer, "Hell, yeah. I'm down. Man, I would love to get out from under TyKita's roof. I mean, I love my sister, but damn she's annoying as fuck."

We shared a laugh and then Feelow said, "Nigga, we bout to knock Marcus off the map with this shit."

"Man, what happened with you and Marcus? I thought y'all were like brothers," I asked because I needed to know what I was stepping into.

Feelow said, "Man, that nigga blew up and forgot those under him. I been with that nigga since sandbox days, and he had the nerve to get Ditto to try to convince me to join him. He tested my loyalty like he ain't trust me or something. He claims he ain't have no part of that, but I know that nigga lying. He told D about my other problem too, because ain't no other way D could have found that out."

"Man, what the fuck you talking about Fee? What problem nigga?" I asked with a curious look on my face.

"Well, since you gon' be pretty much staying here for a minute, I guess you should know, but if I find out you told anybody I'ma kill yo' ass, Tyck. I give you my word on that," Fee stated.

"Dawg, that ass too good for me to turn on. I got yo' back," I said, although, I knew I was gonna stab his ass in the back.

"Man, that long black pipe ain't the only one I like to suck on." He paused and pulled out a glass stem from under a towel on the table and said, "I like to suck on this glass dick, too. This shit keeps my dick hard for hours. You should try it, and then we can get in a real good one."

I had never been curious about drugs and had no desire to try any now or ever so, I passed on his offer. "I'm good you do you, though. I'ma sit back and watch."

Feelow put a piece of hard cocaine on the pipe he held in his hand and as soon as he hit it, his dick rose. When he put the pipe back down, he rubbed on his manhood and said, "Come on over here and sit on this while we discuss how we gon' take that nigga out."

***

I felt it when she looked at me and wondered if she felt it too. I had to act normal, though, because I didn't want Marcus to catch on. She deserved a real nigga on her side, and I needed a good lady to hold me down. I would play it easy for now until I knew for sure that I could pull her away from him. He seemed to have a hold on her, but I was determined to break it.

"So, Marcus, I'm willing to give you the keys for eighteen a piece. You should be able to make a pretty good profit off of that price. Today, I have fifty keys for you. Twenty-five of those on consignment like you asked. I hope fifty is not too much for you and your crew. You sure you can handle that many at once?" I asked as I sold my product.

"Nah, man. I'm good with that amount and the price sounds good too, but how pure is your shit because I'm trying to lock down the whole city and I'm pushing anyone out who ain't down with me," Marcus said with a slight concern in his voice.

"Ya know Marcus, when my father died he passed his crown down to me. I'm not sure if you've done your homework or not, but my father had ties to Escobar, who I'm sure you've heard of. When Escobar was gunned down in the nineties I had yet to be born, but my father made sure that I knew everything about him," I said as the thought of my father made me feel sad, and I took a moment before I continued.

"A man by the name of Don Berna helped bring him down because Escobar killed his bosses, and then he ended up being Escobar's Successor. He ended up running the Medellin Cartel for fifteen years with an even firmer grasp than Pablo or anyone else before him. People feared Berna so much that they even whispered his name while in public because they were afraid his spies would hear them. Ya know, the kids who work for the Colombian Cartels think it's like a life in Hollywood even though, they know that kind of life will eventually lead to their deaths because that is the only way out once in." I looked at Marcus to make sure he was still paying attention. When he didn't comment on my words, I continued, "When cocaine took off in the seventies and eighties, Colombian traffickers sent it directly to the United States and it fell right into my father's hands. They say in Colombia the lowest on the cocaine ladder makes eighty million annually, and I don't know about you Marcus, but that's how I'm trying to live and to keep living even after I pull out for good. Berna is now here in the United States doing thirty-one years because of hos greed, so just because I charge you less than others doesn't mean shit ain't right." I took a breath and continued.

"My product comes straight out of the fields of Catatumbo, but if that's too potent for your customers, I can give it to someone else." I looked at Marcus for his response and right when he was about to give me one, his phone rang.

***

I waited in enjoyment as the dog ripped Ditto's dick completely off his body. His screams of pain were like music to my ears. He had taken the most precious thing I had in my life, so it was only fair that I did the same to him. I had worked beside him for the last ten years and it was hard to wake up every day and not put a bullet in his head. The only thing that stopped me was Paris. I wanted to wait until he got old enough so that he could help me pull it off and feel the relief I felt. "Let's go, Wanda. I got a nice treat for your loyalty. You did wonderful, girl," I said to the pit-bull who dropped the piece of meat from her mouth and trotted over to me. I patted her on the head and then looked over at Ditto and said, "I'll see you in hell, muthafucka." Then Paris put a slug in his chest.

***

I finally heard Feelow pull up outside and said to myself, "Damn, it's about time." Creep looked at me sideways but continued to play the video game. I got up and opened the door for him and saw that he had brought another nigga with him that I didn't recognize. I asked, "Yo, who dis you bringing up in here with you, man?"

"This is Tyck, an old friend of mine and Marcus. We all grew up together, but Tyck got sent up the road when he was fifteen and just came home last week. You gon' be seeing a lot of him, so get use to his face."

Feelow reached out the hand that held the product and when I took it, he said, "This some new shit I want y'all to try out there and see how the fiends take to it."

"What the fuck you mean new shit? Marcus ain't say nothing about no new product. You got me fucked up if you think I'ma sell some shit that Marcus don't know about," I said and tried to pass the bag back, but Creep got up from his game.

He said, "Nah Trap, go ahead and take it. Let's see what we working with." I had been around Creep long enough to know what he was thinking. I knew he wanted to keep the product so we would have something to show Marcus. Proof that Feelow was a snake.

I pulled my hand back and said, "Aiight Fee, we'll try it out, but you better hope that Marcus is cool with this shit."

"Man, me and Marcus got an understanding. He cool dawg, call me when y'all ready to square up," Fee said and then turned to leave. Right before I shut the door behind him he turned and said, "Oh and if I can't make it to pick up my chedda I'ma send my potna here, and if y'all feed him any bullshit we gon' have some issues."

Creep stepped through the door and got in his face and said, "Nigga, you gon' be the only one with issues if we find out some foul shit happening."

I pulled Creep back and said, "We good, Fee. I'll call you when we ready." Then I shut the door and called Marcus.

"Yo, what the fuck you telling me, Trap?" I asked and hoped that I'd heard wrong.

He then repeated himself, "Man, Fee came here with some nigga named Tyck talking about we gon' have to deal with him sometimes and then gave me some new shit to put out. I asked him if you knew about it and he said shit was straight. What you want me to do, man? I ain't going against the grain, dawg. Feelow can kiss my ass."

I was pissed off at what I'd I just heard and knew that I needed to get back home and take care of shit. "Aiight man, good looking out. Let me wrap this shit up and get my ass back down there. Put that shit up and wait on me." Then I hung up.

I looked at B-Line and said, "Man, I ain't gon' be able to stay because some shit bout to go down back home and I need to be there." As soon as I said it, Krystal walked into the room and then another idea crossed my mind. "Aye, why don't I leave my girl here to handle this shit, and I can catch a plane back home. She's less likely to be stopped anyway. You can pack the ride up for her and send her back to me," I said and then looked to Krystal to check for a negative reaction.

B-Line looked from me to her and said, "That's a great plan Marcus, but you sure she cut out for that? We don't want her to get stopped."

I nodded my head and stated, "That white bitch is a soldier and I can assure you, she can handle anything." I walked over to Krystal, wrapped my arms around her, and grabbed her ass.

She awarded me the same affection with her arms around my neck as I asked, "Ain't that right, baby?"

She smiled at me and then pulled back and looked at B-Line and said, "You don't have to worry, Brandon. I can handle it."

"Aiight then, let's finish this up and then y'all can drive me to the airport. Oh, and B, don't try no funny shit with my bitch, nigga. Wouldn't want our business to end before it even gets started good, know what I'm saying?" I warned B-Line as I looked through murderous eyes just to make sure he understood.

Chapter Twenty-One

I remembered those eyes and almost lost my breath because those eyes could put a dent in my story. She was there too when Marcus killed him, but he didn't know it. I happened to look at the window that night as if I felt her looking in. When we made eye contact I should have warned Marcus then, but I was so in shock at what I had witnessed that I couldn't form the words to tell him, but now I had to find a way to get word to him.

After she was removed from the courtroom, the trial continued and every day I searched the seats for Marcus only to be disappointed. I had done so much for him and he didn't have the decency to be here for me. I continued on with my false admission as my heart made up excuses for his absence. On the day of my sentencing, I looked around the courtroom and noticed that Tyck was present. I knew that Marcus wasn't coming and he'd sent Tyck to find out my fate, but still, I couldn't be mad at him or change up. "Would the defendant please rise?" the judge asked and when I stood from my seat he continued, "I hereby sentence you Krystal Madison to serve ten years in the Department of Corrections. You will serve day for day with no time off for good behavior to pay for the life you took." He then looked me deep into my lying eyes and said, "May God have mercy on your soul." He had a look of disappointment on his wrinkled face because he too would have rather sent the young black man I was covering for away for life. But he could kiss my white ass along with anyone else who was against Marcus.

I had sworn to him that I would ride till my death, and I meant it. I would say and do whatever it took to keep Marcus free. I turned and looked Tyck in the eyes and said one name so that he could warn Marcus, and then I was led out of the courtroom and taken to my new home for the next ten years.

***

I hadn't seen Feelow in a couple of days and as soon as he came to my mind, he pulled up in front of me. I didn't know who the nigga was with, but his ass was fine as hell. "Damn, nigga. I thought yo' ass done got ghost on me," I said to Fee as I eyed his passenger up and down.

Fee looked at me sideways and told the man beside him, "Tyck, let that bitch in the car. We about to go have us a good time."

The dude he called Tyck opened the car door and got out so that I could get in. When he pushed the front seat up for me to get in the back, I sucked my teeth and said, "Nigga, queens don't ride in the back seats of anything less than a limo."

Before I could say anything else, Feelow cut in and said, "Yeah, well, when I meet a queen, I'll be sure to pick her up in one. In the meantime, get yo' ass in the backseat unless you want me to go find someone else to entertain me." His comment pissed me off and made me wanna slap the hell out of him, but I knew better than to press my luck, so I kept my mouth shut and got in with an attitude. As soon as Feelow pulled off, he said, "Tyck, lay your seat back so my bitch can top you off real quick."

I spoke up real fast and asked, "Who the fuck are you to tell another nigga I'ma top them off without asking me first?"

"Bitch, you do what I tell you, or I can find a bitch who will. Now lean yo' ass over and make my potna feel good. You know I'm gonna reward yo' ass real proper, so just do it!" Feelow shouted and then looked at his friend.

The man beside him said, "Nah dawg, my shit straight. I got to get back to the crib, anyway. I was only spose' to be going to get Kita some smokes. That bitch probably seething with anger as we speak."

Him saying he was good kinda made me feel rejected, and I didn't take too kindly to that, so I reached around the seat and put my hand over his dick so I could rub it. "Nah, come on. I want Fee to watch me suck anotha niggas dick better than I do his," I said.

He pushed my hand away and stated, "Nah, I said I'm good." I wasn't gonna force his ass, so I just laid back in the seat and crossed my arms. I kept my mouth shut until Feelow finally dropped that nigga's ass off.

I said to myself, *I'ma catch yo' ass solo one day and take that dick.* Then I jumped in the front seat.

***

As soon as I got back into town, I called Trap to come pick me up from the airport. I'd hoped I made the right choice by leaving Krystal behind to handle the run back. I hadn't even known her a full month yet, but every test I put her through was passed with flying colors. This test would be her biggest. I just hoped that B-Line had enough sense not to try me. As soon as I got in the car with Trap, he started telling me all that had been going on.

"So, I found out that Feelow copped some new product from that nigga named Echo," Trap said

"Echo. Man, that nigga had beef with me ever since we were jits about some pussy that I ain't even want. Fee knows that shit too, Dawg. Why the fuck is his ass going against me like this? I ain't understanding this, shit man, FUCK," I said to him with attitude.

"Marcus, I ain't trying to bad talk ya boy or nothing, but that nigga on some flaw shit. Ya know, me and Creep can handle it for you if you can't. We understand that it may be a little harder for you, but we got yo' back," Trap said with sincerity.

I knew that he was referring to killing Feelow, but no matter what, I still had love for the nigga and wasn't ready to count him out just yet.

I told Trap, "Nah, when it gets done, I'm gonna have to be the one to do it. That shit is going to break my heart, but it's something that only I can take care of. But thanks for looking out, though."

Trap then asked, "What about that nigga he brought with him? Said his name was Tyck."

"Yo, let me get up with Tyck and find out what's going on, and I'll get back to you on that. But, for now, I need to run up in something wet, know what I mean," I said to him. I had Trap take me to Netta's house, but when I got there, I didn't get the welcoming I expected.

***

"Hey, y'all got it from here?" I asked my workers as they packed the rear sides of the Expedition with the fifty kilos that Krystal would drive back.

"Yeah Boss, we good," replied Jambo, my number one right hand.

I left him to oversee the project and stepped back in the house to check on the girl and as soon as I walked in she asked, "How long you been doing stuff like this?" Her question caught me off guard, but I was prepared to answer anything for her.

"All my life. This the shit I was born and raised to do," I said and then asked my own question, "How long you been doing niggas like Marcus?"

She looked at me funny and then smiled before she answered, "I met Marcus only a couple of weeks ago and now I'm in too deep to unmeet him."

I walked over closer to her and said, "You're never in too deep to get out. That nigga don't give a fuck about you. What type of man makes his woman travel with fifty kilos of cocaine riding with her?"

"Fuck you. You don't know shit about me, and if I'm correct, you don't know that much about Marcus either. Just finish packing that shit up so I can be on my way," she said and started to walk off.

I grabbed her arm, pulled her back to face me, and said, "I don't have to know you to see that this ain't really what you want to do. I also know that for Marcus to let you traffic his shit after only knowing you for a minute means he doesn't give a fuck about you or my product. Why are you doing it?"

She looked up into my eyes and it melted away any frustration I felt. I wanted to pull her in and never let go. I felt something inside of me shift and knew that I would have to kill Marcus to keep her in my arms. She finally answered me, "I'm doing it because I promised him I'd ride no matter what, and I'm a woman of my word. I'm gonna be who he needs no matter how long I've known him. He plucked me off of the streets and offered me a life to live, so I'm gonna have his back regardless of the consequences. Now get your fuckin hands off of me."

As bad as I wanted to keep my grip on her I knew I couldn't, but I also knew that one day she'd need someone to grasp and I'd be waiting. "Remember this number and if you ever need anything or anyone you call it, even if it's five years from now. I'll make sure it never changes," I said and then whispered a phone number in her ear, and then I let her go.

***

"We did it, son. We finally did it. That bastard got what he deserved," I said to Paris when we left the warehouse.

"Yeah Pops, that shit is finally over. I know moms rejoicing right now. Did you see how Wanda tore his dick off? Ah, that shit was funny. Man, we should have recorded it and charged the niggas a fee to watch. Whoo, we would have made a fortune!" Paris yelled as he celebrated our victory."The time is coming and now we gon' take some shit over and change the whole game. What you think about that, son?" I looked over at him and was proud of who he'd become. Paris was a street nigga like me with a heart full of compassion like his momma.

"I been waiting on this all my life. Our crew, along with Marcus' crew are gonna make it to where the whole city eats," Paris said with a smile.

Me and Paris wanted to change the game, so everybody would be able to enjoy the wealth. We knew that getting rid of Ditto would not only avenge Towanda's death, but it would also bring a sense of peace to the streets. The whole hood had feared Ditto, but he would no longer reign on these streets. The freedom of being out of his grasp would make it easier for me to love again, and I knew just whose heart I would try to get in.

***

I opened my eyes and my hands went straight to my neck. It felt like his hands were still around it and I struggled to breathe. I realized that he may still be there for a minute. I waited and heard nothing, so I slowly got up and ran into the kitchen to get the gun that Milo had kept hidden in there. I made sure it was loaded and then walked room to room to make sure I was alone. When I saw that I was, I put the gun down and breathed a sigh of relief. "Oh, my GOD. Oh, my GOD. What am I gonna do without you, Milo?" I stated aloud as the tears begin to fall from my eyes. I then heard a noise and picked the gun back up.

I slowly walked back into the living room with the gun leading my way and walked into Marcus. "Yo. Yo Netta, chill. It's just me. Put that shit down!" he cried out, but his words fell on deaf ears. I proceeded to walk closer to him and he slowly backed up while he held his hands out in front of him and said, "Netta, it's me Marcus. What the fucks going on? Chill with that gun."

I finally found the courage to speak, "Is it true, Marcus? Is it true you muthafucker?" I asked as I looked deep into his eyes.

He asked, "What the fuck you talking bout, Netta? Why don't you put the gun down, and we can talk about whatever it is."

I shook my head and asked one more time, "Did you kill Milo? Did you? Just tell me the truth, Marcus. Did you take him from us?"

He put his hands down and then sat on the couch like I wasn't holding a gun on him and then told me the story, "Yeah Netta, I did kill Milo, but Ditto didn't give me much of a choice. Milo started smokin' that shit and was taking from the pot. Ditto wasn't happy about it and since I brought him into the mix I had to do the work." He paused and stood back up and then said, "I didn't want to do it, but I had to because if Ditto would have ordered someone else to do it Milo would have suffered. You gotta understand my position here."

I went against my better judgement and lowered the gun. I said, "He was all me and Lil Milo had, Marcus. How the fuck could you do that to us? You were supposed to be his friend and you took him from us, you bastard." I raised the gun from behind. Before I could turn my head to see what it was, something hit me and the room went black.

***

"Yo sis, I need to borrow your car for a minute. I got a job interview and don't wanna be late," I said to Kita. I would tell her later on about me planning to stay with Feelow for a while because I had other things to take care of.

"A job interview? Where you got an interview at, Tyckori?" she asked with an attitude.

"Damn. I'll tell you if I get the job, but I don't wanna jinx myself, so can I get the keys or not?" I asked as I held my hand out for her keys, she looked at me crazy and then went into her purse and pulled them out.

When she threw them at me she said, "And yo' ass betta come straight back with my shit, too." Then I turned around and slammed the door behind me.

I knew that Feelow would be gone a while, so it was the perfect opportunity to go back and see Trap so I could tell him my plan to set up Feelow. When I pulled up to the bottom, Trap walked out with a burner in his hand and stated, "I don't remember asking Fee to send you by, so why the fuck are you here?"

I walked up closer to the porch and said, "Trap, I know we don't know each other, but I'm on your side, dawg. Just let me come in and talk to you for a minute."

"Why the fuck should I do that? Where that snake nigga Feelow at anyway?" Trap asked as he looked toward the car I had driven.

I replied, "Fee picked up some trick bitch named Keisha and took her to the motel. He don't even know I'm here. I just wanna talk to you to see if you wanna help me set that nigga up. He trying to take Marcus out, but I fuck with Marcus the long way and I ain't gonna let that shit happen. I'm only hanging with Fee to try to find out his plan. I let the nigga suck my dick and all just to get in." I laughed and then said, "Muthafucka must have tasted good to him cause now he wants my ass to crash at his crib."

Trap put the gun in his waistband and said, "Yo man, I don't want to hear no homo shit. I been caught on to his punk ass, I just ain't said nothing." He paused and stepped to the side and said, "Come on in, but if you make one wrong move, I'ma blast your ass."

Before he let me go all the way in, he patted me down for a weapon, but I knew better than to carry. I had just got out of prison and wasn't trying to go back for a weapon possession. I'd die in the streets first. I asked Trap before I went any further, "We good now?"

He nodded his head and we walked inside. I asked as soon as I got inside, "Where ya boy at? He gonna want to hear this, too."

"He had something else he needed to go handle, but he'll be back soon. I'll update him if it's that important," Trap said in a flat voice. I could tell that my presence wasn't welcome, but once I caught him up on what was happening, he'd leave his door open for me from then on.

"Aiight, you are all packed up and ready so I guess until next time, you be careful driving back," B-Line said out of concern. Then added, "You don't have to do this if you don't want to. That nigga ain't gon' do shit about it."

B-Line seemed to be more worried about me than his product and I ain't gonna lie, I was scared as hell, but I was determined to do this for Marcus. I said, "Marcus needs me to do this, so you shouldn't worry so much." I had to be hard because if I didn't I could very well fall weak for him. I could feel the pull, but I continued to push, hoping to stop it. Marcus saved my life, and trafficking his dope was the least I could do.

The couple of days I'd spent in Baltimore with B-Line were peaceful and although I enjoyed myself, I knew I had to leave. I didn't want to start any unnecessary drama. "Thanks for everything, Bradoon. I'll see you on the next trip," I said, and then left him as he stood there hoping I'd change my mind.

***

"Yo man, what the fuck?" I asked Creep when he put a bullet between Netta's eyes.

He looked at me with murder embedded in his soul and said, "Dawg, that bitch found out you killed Milo. It was you or her."

"Good lookin' out, man. How that bitch find that shit out?" I asked. Curious because only my closest niggas knew the truth.

Creep said what I'd wished he'd kept to himself, "Fee left here not too long ago. I was coming over to talk to this bitch about them eight G's although, I already know she ain't touch it. I saw his car, so I parked a little ways down the street and waited. When he pulled out, you pulled in not long after. No one else has been here."

I stood there a minute and thought about what Creep said before I spoke again. "I hate to think that my nigga sold me out like that. Man, the shit he doing just ain't adding up to me. I haven't done shit to make him act like this. Ever since Ditto called him over, he been acting funny." I paused and laughed to myself and said to Creep as I looked in his eyes, "Ya know, he thought I got Ditto to try his ass by testing his loyalty and shit, but I ain't never questioned that." I looked to the floor where Netta laid with her eyes permanently closed because of Feelow's betrayal. My heart broke at the thought. Creep interrupted my thoughts and said, "Boss, I'ma call the clean-up crew. You go on and head home so you can clear your head. When you ready to make a move, me and Trap got you."

I looked at Creep and said, "Yeah, I'ma go and let you handle this. Make sure somebody gets some bread over to Netta's grandmother for Lil Milo. We got to take care of him now because when he gets older, he's gonna want to know who took his parents out. We need him on our side to ensure that he don't find out the truth."

I started to shut the door behind me, but turned around and said, "Yo Creep, tell Trap I'll make contact soon, and I'll send some work over as soon as my girl gets back. Until then, sit on that shit Fee gave y'all. I'm gonna need it to feed back to him." Then I walked out.

Chapter Twenty-Two

"Who the fuck was that nigga, Feelow?" I asked because I'd never seen him before.

Feelow disrespectful as always said, "It don't matter who he was. The only thing you need to worry about is this dick. Now bring yo' fine ass here and show me how much you missed me."

I put my hands on my hips and stated, "So you was just gon' make me suck anotha nigga dick like that."

He reached his hand out, pulled me to him, and then smiled. Then he said, "I just wanted to see you do it, baby. You so damn sexy when you got them pretty ass lips around the head of my dick, so I wanted to see was they just as pretty around another one. That shit would have had me on swole."

I laughed at him and then asked him what I'd been wondering, "When you plan on making a move on Marcus?" I couldn't wait to help him set Marcus up. I hated that bastard and had been mad at him ever since he'd dissed me. I also wanted him back inside of me. I'd planned to ride that dick real good until Feelow handled his ass.

"Damn girl, you act like you wanna get rid of his ass worse than me. What's up with that?" Feelow asked, and I told him the truth.

"I still feel some type of way about how he dissed me, and I can't wait for you to sit his ass down. He acted like I wasn't good enough for him. You the real boss, Feelow. You need to hurry up and let the streets know that."

"The times coming soon, Keisha. Just be patient. In the meantime, I got some new shit I want to try, and then I'ma tear that pussy up," he said as he fixed me a hit on his pipe. He passed it to me and watched as I put it to my lips, and then he lit the tip of it for me. I inhaled and as soon as the smoke filled my lungs, I vomited.

I found the strength to open my eyes and as soon as I did, the pain shot through my body. I looked around and tried to figure out where I was but didn't recognize the place. When I tried to get up the pain pushed me back down. "Aah. Ah, shit," I cried out on the verge of tears. "Where the hell am I?" I asked myself out loud and then heard a noise right before another figure appeared before me.

"Shhh. Don't move. You don't have the strength yet. Here, I brought you something to put on your stomach," she said with a sincere look on her face. She then propped my back up on some pillows.

With a confused look on my face, I asked, "Where the hell am I?" Instead of answering, she tried to feed me the hot liquid from the bowl she held, so I asked again, "Dammit, where the hell am I and how did I get here?"

She placed the bowl down and replied, "You're safe and that's all you should worry about until you get your strength back." I then recalled my ordeal and my hands immediately went to my dick which was covered in bandages except for the very tip. I sighed in relief and stated, "Oh thank goodness. Shit. I thought….."

"You thought right, Dittrick. I had a surgeon come in and reattach it. Once it heals completely you should have all of the feeling back. There will be some scars, but it's not as bad as you thought. All of it is still there."

I found it hard to understand why she was helping me, so I asked out of curiosity. "Why are you helping me? I've treated you like shit my entire life and yet you're here now saving me."

With tears in her eyes she answered, "You only lived by what your father taught you, and I just couldn't give up on my son and I love you."

I thought for a minute and said, "I got to get to Stone and Paris. They did this shit to me. I'ma kill those muthafuckers."

She nodded her head and replied, "I know who did it, son, but you shouldn't worry about them right now. You just concentrate on getting well and when the time is right, I'll bring them straight to you."

***

The ride back from Baltimore seemed longer than the ride there. Perhaps because I was fifty kilos heavier. I hoped that doing this for

Marcus would make him more attentive to me and my feelings. I knew that he was still fucking other bitches though he wouldn't ever admit it.

I could still feel Brandon's presence but tried to push him out of my thoughts. I knew Marcus would kill him if he knew what he'd said, but I was far from a snitch and would never tell.

When I pulled in and parked, I sat there a minute before I got out. I breathed a sigh of relief, thankful that I'd made it back safely. I walked to the door and when I opened it I'd hoped that Marcus would be there to greet me, but instead, I stepped into loneliness, a feeling that was all too familiar.

"Damn Marcus, you leaving?" she asked as I got up and put my clothes on. I'd finished what I came to do so there was no sense in hanging around. I also needed to get back home because I knew Krystal would be back soon.

"Yeah, I'm leaving what the hell I need to stay for? Shit, I got what I came for," I said.

She sucked her teeth at me and said, "You a cold muthafucka, Marcus. And one day somebody is gonna heat yo ass up." I paid the bitch no attention and walked out.

When I pulled up to my place and parked, I noticed that Krystal had already made it back and smiled. *"I knew your ass was gonna come in handy,"* I said to myself and then got out.

She was at the door waiting when I got to it and asked with an attitude, "Why the fuck you ain't answer your phone when I tried to call you?" I don't know why dick makes females act like they own you, but this white bitch had me fucked up.

I got in her face and said, "Didn't I tell yo ass about questioning me? I don't answer to you or any muthafuckin body else. Now come here and show a nigga some love."

I put my arms around her because I knew I needed to show her some affection. It was the least I could do after she'd just risk her life and freedom for me. I tried to butter her up by saying, "Baby, I was just out handling some business. Damn, I missed you. A nigga happy to see yo pretty ass." I put her hand on my dick and asked," You goin' to give daddy some of that wet pussy tonight? Huh?" She finally smiled and started to pull off her clothes. I closed the front door, so I could reward her. I needed to make things right because I'd need her to do another run really soon.

***

"Bitch, what the fuck is wrong with you?" I hollered and pushed Keisha away from me. The hit I'd put on the pipe for her was big, but I didn't expect her to get sick from it.

She wiped her mouth and looked up at me and said, "Damn Feelow, that shit potent as fuck." I was mad at her for vomiting on me, but I charged it to the dope.

"Maybe I should put a little cut on it before I put it out there. I don't need people getting sick off my shit. Nah, I need them motherfuckers to feel good and enjoy themselves, so they'll come back for more," I said to her.

Keisha got up off the bed and went into the bathroom to clean herself up. I followed behind her, but something in my gut told me that it wasn't the dope that caused her to get sick.

***

For the next few weeks, Marcus treated me like a queen and caused me to fall deeper in love with him. He schooled me on all the things I needed to know about the streets, along with all the tricks I needed to know in the bedroom. I thought that maybe something inside of him had changed and would cause him to be more respectful of me, but I would be far from right.

I was in the middle of giving him some slow head when his cell phone rang, "Sup?" he asked the caller when he answered and a second later he pushed me off of him and sat up, "Where the fuck is he at then?" he asked. He listened for a couple of minutes and then said, "Nah, I'm coming and, Fee, don't go nowhere. Wait for me there."

After he hung up, he sat there for a minute and then turned to me and said, "I gotta go meet my boy. Seems that Ditto ain't been seen in weeks and can't nobody find him. Feelow's at his house with a couple of his crew members now." He paused and got up to get dressed and then looked at me and said, "I need you to be on the road within the next two hours. The truck's already packed up and ready to go. B-Line will be expecting you."

I sighed out of disappointment but got up and hopped in the shower. After I turned the water on and got lathered up, I hopped back out and asked Marcus, "What happens if one day I get caught doing shit?"

He laughed to himself and said, "Then you do your time and pretend you don't know me." Then he walked out.

***

I listened closely at the conversation that Echo, Swag T, and Toe Tag had. They'd picked me up to have some fun but didn't know that I fucked with Marcus and his crew. I sucked Toe Tags dick slowly, so I wouldn't miss a word. "We gotta keep that nigga Feelow on our good side until we can get to Marcus. We gon' hit all his traphouses first and then bam, take his ass out." He then put his hand on the back of my head and said, "Yeah bitch, suck this dick. Pretty soon, I'ma have that white bitch of Marcus' on this muthafucka. Yeah, shit."

Swag T stood up and said, "Man, I wish yo ass would hurry the hell up and nut, so I can get mine too. Damn, you taking forever, dawg."

"Man, that bitch don't wanna suck on that rant ass pussy you got," Echo said as he sat to the side and counted money.

All three of them shared a laugh and when Toe Tag finally came in my mouth Swag T said, "Come on here, lil mama, and suck on a real piece of meat." She laughed and then handed me a piece of dope to smoke before I started. While I took a minute to hit my piece, I heard Toe Tag's phone ring.

He answered it and said to the person on the other end, "Good job. If that nigga don't get the message and surrender it all to us, we'll just hit another one." Then he hung up.

Toe Tag looked at Swag T and then to Echo and said, "Boys, just hit Datsun. They on the way to the meet up spot with the money and drugs. One down my niggas." They would have to leave to meet up with whoever ToeTag had talked to but was quickly disappointed.

Swag T said, "Come on and take care of me before we gotta jet."

When I got between her legs, I couldn't concentrate because all I heard was Marcus' name over and over in my head. My only mission was to make this bitch nut and hoped that I could make it before another one of his crew was eliminated.

***

I hadn't seen Feelow in a couple of weeks, but when I walked into Ditto's home, it was as if there was tension between us. We gave each other some dap and then I asked him, "How long has it been since that nigga's been seen?"

Feelow shook his head and replied, "Point Blank said him and Tray Pop been blowing that niggas phone up to get some more work, but he ain't answered none of they calls."

"Maybe that nigga skipped town for a minute. You know he always on some secret mission," I said and then got lost in thought before I asked, "What about Stone? Don't tell me that nigga ghost, too."

Feelow didn't have to respond because his look alone gave me my answer. We walked further into the home and then Feelow broke the silence once again. "They said that Stone been missing in action too. Something ain't right man."

"Yeah, I see that." I looked Feelow in the eyes and said, "Man, I know we ain't been right lately, but we gotta pull together and find out where these niggas at. Are you still fuckin with Echo and his set?"

"Dawg, I don't deal with that nigga no more. His ass tried to snake me on my cut, so I finished paying him off and told him to kiss my ass. I've just been waiting for the right time to get up with you and hopefully make amends," Feelow stated, but for some reason I felt like it was all a lie. However, we needed to get along for the sake of the streets.

I said to him, "Man, you neva should have let the thought of me setting you up cross your mind. You my brotha and I'd never do no shit like that to you."

He nodded his head and replied, "Yeah man, I know. I think that shit had me paranoid, but I see clearly now. I'm sorry I went against the grain for a minute. I hope we good now."

Before I could answer him my phone rang and when I answered it, I didn't expect what I heard coming from the other end. "Aiight, thanks for letting me know." I hit the end button and looked up into Feelow's curious eyes and told him the bad news, "Datsun's just been hit."

***

"So how long you gonna do this for him?" I asked her curiously. She hesitated with her answer and when she finally spoke, her voice was broken.

"I-I guess as long as he needs me to. What other choice do I have, Brandon? I told you the story, and now I know too much. I'm in too deep. He'll never let me go." Her beauty and innocence captivated me and all I needed her to do was say the word, and I'd cut the ties she had with Marcus. I could see the pain in her eyes and pulled her close to me. She started to cry and said, "I just want him to love me, Brandon, but he's too busy loving other women. What's wrong with me?"

"Not a damn thing and don't ever forget that. He doesn't deserve you," I said and then put my lips to hers. I thought that she'd resist, but instead, she welcomed my affection.

I instantly got hard and when our kiss broke, she said, "Make love to me, Brandon."

I brushed a finger over her cheek and said, "I don't want to take advantage of you while you're like this, Krystal. You're just vulnerable right now, and I don't want you to do something you may regret just because you're mad at him."

She pulled her shirt off over her head and then unsnapped her bra and said, "No, this is what I want to do. Not because I'm mad at him, but because of how you make me feel." She took a breath and then said, "You make me feel like somebody. You're like my shelter from the storm. Please, Brandon." I wanted to reject her offer because I knew that when we were done, she would return to Marcus, but I couldn't resist her. I picked her up in my arms, carried her upstairs to my bedroom, and gave her body something I knew Marcus never would.

***

"You're as beautiful as ever, Delores," he said and caused me to blush a little.

I said in a voice that sounded more like a love-struck teenager than a grown woman, "Oh Stone, get outta here. You just trying to make me feel good."

"No. I've felt like this for a while, but I knew Ditto would never allow us to be together," he said and then asked with fake concern in his voice, "Speaking of Ditto. Have you seen him lately? He seems to have went AWOL."

I replied, "Ah, Stone. You know that my son doesn't tell me anything about what's going on in his life. He hates me for killing that bastard of a sperm donor he called his father. I'm sure he's okay. Maybe he went away to get a peace of mind."

I then asked, "How do you think he would feel knowing his Lieutenant has a crush on me?"

Stone laughed and responded, "I would hope that I've been in his life long enough for him to accept it, regardless of how he feels about you. I'm only about ten years older than him, but he's like a son to me. Plus, I'm grown and don't need his permission. Now what's up?"

Stone played right into my hands, so I knew I had to keep going. "I haven't been intimate with a man since I've been sober and I know that hasn't been long, but if I could be with any man I'd want it to be you." I pulled him in closer to me and then said, "When we're done, we can look for my son together."

***

When me and Marcus pulled up to the spot that Datsun had been hit at, we jumped out of the car immediately. We were met by Blow and C-John, who were calmer than I could have imagined, Blow said, "The neighbors said he was just coming back from the store for his momma and a tan colored box Chevy passed by and started popping off. They said it happened so fast that they couldn't identify the shooter. I got people out looking for the ride, but you already know how that's going to turn out."

C-John cut in, "Yo Marcus, his momma ain't taking it too well. You need to go in and check on her, dawg."

Marcus then looked to me and said, "Yo Fee, hold it down out here. I'ma go in and check on Ma B."

I nodded my head to let him know it was all good and as soon as he walked off, Trap and Creep walked up. Creep asked me, "Yo Fee, you don't know nothing 'bout this hit my nigga?"

I looked at him with angered eyes and said, "Seems like you trying to imply something. Be straight up, Creep. Something you wanna say, my man? Perhaps you can enlighten us all and spit out what you talking about."

Creep shook his head and walked off, leaving me and Trap alone. Trap said, "Word on the street is that this was an Echo hit! Ain't that the nigga you running with now?"

I shook my head and looked away before I spoke, "Nah, I cut my ties with Echo. That was a mistake I'll never make again. Me and Marcus cool, but last time I checked you answer to me, not the other way around. So stay in your fucking place. As a matter of fact, take yo ass out in them streets and see what you can find out about this shit."

Trap stared at me like I was crazy and then said, "Yeah, I'm on it, but maybe you need to inform Marcus of how many crew members he's gonna end up losing because of yo' snake ass." Then he walked away.

***

"Pregnant. Bitch, what the fuck you mean pregnant?" I asked the nurse at the clinic. I couldn't believe my ears and wondered what the fuck I was gonna do. I had been fucking so many niggas that I couldn't determine who I was pregnant by. The last time I was with Feelow and had gotten sick, I decided that I needed to get a checkup. I was so busy tricking in the streets that I had neglected my health. I thought I might have caught a venereal disease or something, but never expected to be told I was gonna have a baby. I knew in the back of my mind just who I would pin this baby on. I only hoped he would accept it.

I picked up the phone and dialed Feelow's number. It rang a few times before he picked up and when he did, he had a straight attitude. "What the fuck you want, Keisha? We just lost one of our crew members, so I'm not in the mood for yo shit."

I wondered what had happened, but didn't want to ask too many questions, so instead I said, "I just called to give you some news that may cheer you up. Feelow, I'm pregnant. That's why I had gotten sick."

There was a long pause as if he were thinking about what I'd just said and then he stated, "Well, what the fuck you telling me for? You betta call that lil muthafuckas daddy 'cause bitch it ain't mine."

I could not believe that he had the audacity to say some shit like that to me. I snapped back, "You the only nigga I been giving this to, Feelow. So, stop trippin." I'd hoped he'd believe me, but Feelow knew more about me than I thought he did.

He said, "Bitch, I wish you was standing in front of me right now, so I could slap yo' lying ass. Just remember that niggas talk. Now you need to figure out who its daddy is, so you can see what he wants to do about it. When you get rid of that lil muthafucker let me know and I'll come scoop you up and fill you with this dick. It's your choice, but my ass ain't claiming no seeds." Then he hung up in my ear.

"You fucking piece of shit," I said out loud and slammed the phone down on the hook. I knew the rest of the niggas I had fucked would turn me away because they all had a main chic, so I was basically on my own. There was no way I could raise a baby without help. I sold my pussy for a living to the drug dealers who needed a quick nut, so I was in no position to feed another mouth. I decided to tell one of the other men that it was their baby and ask for the money to get an abortion before I ran my ass back to Feelow.

***

When I made it back home with another shipment for Marcus, he was in a foul mood. He seemed to have a lot on his mind so I tried to stay out of his way, but he wanted to take his frustration out on me. "Get undressed and lay yo' ass down."

I asked him in a confused voice, "Marcus, why are you acting like this to me?" My words fell on deaf ears as he rammed himself inside of me. "Marcus, stop you're hurting me." I tried to push him off of me, but the harder I pushed the more aggressive he became.

"Bitch, just lay there and take this shit. I just need to release some pressure right now, so take it like a real woman." Then he collapsed on top of me.

I could tell that he was tipsy, but I didn't think it was enough to make him pass out. His weight was heavy on my small frame and it took me a few minutes to maneuver myself from under him. When I finally did, I heard his cell ring and instinct made me pick it up and answer, "Hello."

There was silence for a minute and then I heard a voice ask, "Where's Marcus?"

I answered them, "Um, Marcus is asleep. I can give him a message when he wakes up, though."

The man on the other end, then said in a stern voice, "Nah, wake his ass up now and tell him that Montell just got murked." Then he hung up.

***

Paris was really fucked up about Montell's murder, and the streets wasn't talking. I called a meeting with the entire crew, and also with the crew that Ditto had left hanging from his disappearing act. He still hadn't been seen or heard from in weeks, but we now had other shit to handle, so looking for him was put on the back burner.

When everyone made it to the warehouse, I gave Feelow the floor. "Now that we are all together, we have to come up with a plan. Our people are slowly being taken out by an unknown force-"

Tray Pop cut in and said, "Yeah, Fee. They say that force is your dawg Echo and his team. Is that true?"

Feelow thought about the question before he responded, "I been cut ties with him and his crew and as far as I know, that nigga left town and went back to Brooklyn where his ass came from. My loyalty is here with y'all and Marcus."

Paris spoke up, "Yeah, I guess with loyalty like yours, a muthafucka don't need no enemies."

"Look, Fee made a mistake, but that shit is the past and we gon' let it go and move on. We need to focus on arming ourselves and getting out in them streets. We gon' eliminate any muthafucka that looks at us sideways," I said. Then added, "I hooked up with Temple and got us some heavy artillery, so I want everyone to come up here and pick out the gun of your choice. We bout to make these streets bleed until we get justice for our men." I took a breath and looked around the room before I continued, "Is there anyone in here who ain't willing to fight for the team? If so, get yo' ass up now and walk the fuck out, but don't ever come back." When no one moved, I nodded my head at Tyck who then pulled out the duffle bag full of guns. Movement and chatter filled the room right before Stone walked in.

***

When I walked in, all eyes were upon me as if they'd seen a ghost. I looked around the room to locate who I'd come for and when I saw him, I walked straight over to him. "Son, I'm so sorry. I just heard about Montell," I said, as I embraced Paris.

"Son, what the hell?" Blackout asked with a look of confusion on his face.

Paris pulled from my embrace and said to everyone, "Yeah, this is my father. I'll explain everything at a better time."

I turned to the front of the room, where Marcus and Feelow stood at a table filled with heavy artillery. When I looked in their eyes, they lowered the weapons they held in their hands. Marcus asked me, "Does Ditto know about this?"

I replied proudly, "What Ditto knows doesn't matter anymore. My son and I made sure of that." I paused and looked around the room to see if I got a reaction from any of his men. When I didn't, I continued, "We're the reason that he is missing." The room erupted in a loud chatter, but when Paris held his hand up everyone got quiet, and then we told them the story.

Chapter Twenty-Three

I crossed my arms and sat back in the chair so I could watch Feelow. No one knew about our rendezvous, but honestly, I wouldn't have gave a fuck. A nigga shouldn't be worried about my sexual preference unless they willing to indulge in it. I was actually impressed with the way Feelow handled himself but wondered how many of them niggas really listened to him. I wasn't that familiar with anyone there, but Marcus and Feelow and now Trap and Creep. Marcus recruited me to the set as extra muscle and put me over the weapons. I enjoyed the show as they picked through the artillery that was laid out on the table. A gun could tell you a lot about a muthfucka's personality, so I sat there and read everyone in the room.

Marcus noticed me as I sat to the side by myself, and then he came over to talk to me. When he walked up and asked, "What's going on, Tyck? You lookin like you got a lot of shit riding around in that head of yours right now."

I smiled a one-sided smile and said, "Ya know what? You my boy, Marcus. So, I want you to always remember that I got your back at all costs." He listened hard but continued to watch his crew. I said, "You do know that when it's time to take care of Feelow, I can handle it for you. I know that shits gonna be hard for you, Dawg."

He turned to me with a look of sadness in his eyes and said, "I 'preciate it man, but its gonna have to be me that does it. I know how hard it may be for me, it's gonna get done."

I uncrossed my arms and leaned my elbows on to my knees and said, "Aiight. But, if you end up needing me, don't hesitate to call." I patted Marcus on the back and then got up, so I could manage the weapons and document in my mind who picked out what. When I caught Feelow's stare and when he nodded his head, my dick got hard.

***

The streets went silent for a minute, but I kept my men on high alert just in case someone was in the shadows waiting for them to relax their guns and get comfortable. Me and Feelow had made it through his disloyalty, but I kept a close eye on him because I still couldn't find a way to completely trust him again. He wasn't aware that I knew about his and Tyck's shit, but that shit wasn't a secret except to Feelow himself and to tell the truth, I really didnt give a fuck.

My business with B-Line had increased because with Ditto gone and his weak ass dope gone, the fiends were bringing that cheddar three-fold. I looked to my right side and watched as Krystal slept peacefully. I had thought about treating her more respectfully because she had proven herself, but I wasn't willing to give up all those other bitches. Shit, a nigga needed some variety in his life and wasn't trying to settle with one piece.

I heard my phone buzz as it sat on the nightstand and picked it up before it woke Krystal up. "Yo, what's up?" I asked without looking to see who the caller was and heard, "Hello, you have a collect call from,(beep) Carlos Johnson, an inmate at The County Jail Facility. To accept the call, press one now. To refuse the…." I pressed one to accept the call and asked C-John as soon as it went through, "Yo C, what the fuck happened, man? Why you calling from the county jail?"

C-John said in his deep baritone, "Man Marcus, my ass got popped coming off the Amtrak with fifteen ounces and a burner. Nigga, I need you to come get me." I felt the white girl beside me begin to move and turned my head to look at her.

I asked C-John, "What's that bond looking like, man?"

He replied, "Fifty G's, Dawg, but you know I got you. Just don't make me stay up in this bitch too long."

I laughed, although the situation wasn't a funny one. I teased his big ass and said, "Let me find out your ass is scared and shit."

"Nah, a nigga ain't scared bout nothing, but they some bigger muthafuckas in here bigger than me and they lookin at my ass like it's gon be they next meal. I ain't trying to catch no murder charges too, but if one of these bitches try me I'ma bust they wig open. You know this my first time in da joint, man," C-John stated.

"Aiight, just chill. I'll get the money together and send my girl to the bondsman," I said and looked at Krystal who looked back at me with her big green eyes. I shrugged my shoulders at her and said into the phone, "Look for a pretty ass white girl when they release you. She'll be driving the Ex-p. Oh and nigga, don't try my bitch." Then I hung up.

Only Feelow and Tyck had met Krystal because I had chosen to keep her away from those other thirsty ass niggas. However, only Tyck knew that she was still around. Because of Feelow's disloyalty, I made him think that I had kicked her to the curb once I got what I wanted and I planned to keep it that way. I knew that I should have probably told my whole crew about her, especially because of situations like the one C-John had gotten himself into, but I also wanted to keep her safe so she wouldn't be touched. "I need for you to go down to the jail and get one of my boy's out," I said to her in a calm voice.

"Marcus, why can't you go get him? I don't even know who he is," she stated.

"Because I told yo ass to go get him, that's why. Look, if you going to continue to ride with me then you gotta understand that you going to have to step up to the plate sometimes and swing the bat. That time is now, so I need you to get up and go get Carlos. You feel what I'm saying, or do I have to make you?" I declared.

"Yes Marcus, you know I'm gonna do it. Where do I take him after I pick him up?" she asked me and I replied in a stern voice.

"Wherever the fuck he tells you to take him and bring yo pretty ass right back home." Something in my gut told me not to send her, but I went against my better judgement because I had a phobia with jails and prisons. She got up and got dressed so she could do as I asked. I sat back on the bed to watch her and my dick instantly rose. I licked my lips and said, "Look what your ass do to me. I ain't neva had a bitch that could make my dick perk up by watching them put fucking clothes on, that's why I ain't neva letting your ass go."

She walked over to the bed and stared me down, then ran a finger over the tip of my dick to smear the pre-cum. She then put the finger in her mouth and sucked the juice off of it.

Right before she walked out and slammed the door, she hollered out, "Oh yeah, Marcus. I forgot to tell you, I'm pregnant!"

***

"Look man, we done chilled for a minute now. I think it's time to resurface and pull that shit right out from under his ass. Feelow say that nigga bringing in work that comes straight from the fields of Colombia. He said them fiends is losing they minds over that shit," Swag T said, trying to convince me that it was time to make another move on Marcus.

I looked at my baby sister and said, "Nah, T. I still think we should wait until we find out whose making his pick-ups and where they makin' them at."

Swag T responded in an excited yet impatient manner, "Man, that nigga ain't gon' let Feelow know when and where them pickups come about. Shit, he said Marcus won't even settle down with one bitch because he too afraid someone would use her to get to him."

The door suddenly swung open and Toe Tag walked in with some pizza and two six packs and a big ass smile on his face, so I asked, "Nigga, why you walk up in this bitch cheesin? You acting like you just pulled out of some bomb ass pussy."

Toe Tag replied, "Nah, man. I brought pizza and beer, so we can celebrate."

Me and Swag looked at him like he was crazy and then I asked, "What the fuck we 'pose to be celebrating? Don't tell me your ass finally graduated sixth grade." Me and Swag shared a laugh while Toe Tag popped open a cold one and threw the top at me.

He shook his head, picked up his cell phone, tossed it to me, and said, "Take a look at that."

I looked at the picture on the phone and then passed it to Swag and asked, "She pretty, but why you got me looking at that snow bunny? Am I 'pose to know who she is or something?" Toe Tag smiled his crooked smile one more time and looked me right in the eyes, and then he told me her identity.

***

"I think that I should make my move soon," Feelow said out loud as I lay beside him in bed.

"What move you talking 'bout Fee?" I asked. He sat up and threw the sheets off of himself before he stood. His early morning erection stared me in the face, but I knew a head job wasn't what was on his mind.

He replied, "I think it's time to hook back up with Echo and go through with our plan to move on Marcus. That nigga got millions stashed and is living like a fucking king somewhere in a hidden location. That's supposed to be my boy and I've known that muthafucka all my life and yet, I don't even know where he lays his head at."

Feelow sat back down on the bed and I got up and sat beside him. I thought for a minute and then spoke, "Aiight, you know I got your back. What you need me to do?" I needed him to tell me his mission before he started to tell me, his cell phone rang.

***

"Damn, yo' ass sho' is pretty. Marcus wasn't lying. What's up? I'm Carlos," he stated and then extended his hand to me.

I smiled at his courtesy and said, "Hi, nice to meet you. I'm Krystal and thanks for the compliment. Come on, I parked in the back like Marcus told me to." Carlos followed me out of the door, and together we walked to the Expedition that was more my ride now than Marcus'.

I got in and pressed the button to release the locks on the doors, but before Carlos could reach out and grab the handle a figure ran up behind him and shot him in the back of the head. I tried not to panic, although, it was hard, but Marcus had trained me for situations like this. I hurried and pressed the heightened security button that was hidden under the leather of the driver's seat and the vehicle automatically changed to bullet proof. The man that had shot Carlos grabbed the door handle, but it shocked him with a few bolts of electricity and caused him to pull back stunned. I put the Expedition in reverse and backed out as quickly as I could. "Shit, shit, shit!" I hollered out loud and then sped off.

I looked in my rearview mirror to make sure no one got behind me, and a little further down the road I pulled into an underground parking garage. I sat there a minute so I could catch my breath, and before I pulled back out I hit the camouflage button which instantly made the ride change colors and tinted the windows. It also flipped new tags on to the front and rear bumpers. When I pulled out of the garage space, I fell into heavy traffic and called Marcus.

***

"Why you ain't tell me about the white girl, nigga?" You spose to let me in on everything if you want this shit to play out right," Echo said into the phone when I answered.

I replied, "Yo man. That muthafucka told me he got rid of that bitch and I ain't seen her with him since he brought her to my crib. How you find out about her anyway?"

"Let's just say I got niggas on my team that do they fucking homework. I don't like not knowing something when I have my eyes on a target to get at. I'm not too fond of surprises, Feelow," Echo said angrily. I held my head down and felt Tyck walk up behind me. I lifted a finger to my lips so he wouldn't say anything. I didn't want Echo to know I had company.

"Man, I swear I didn't know. We'd found that bitch in an alley all dirty and shit months ago. He ain't say nothing about keeping her."

"It's all good. I sent my boy out to try and get his hands on her. Ya know, one of ya'lls set got popped coming off the Amtrak. Marcus sent the white girl to bond him out. It's a shame that nigga ain't neva make it to court," Echo stated and then added, "When I get my hands on that porcelain doll I'ma break her limb by limb till that nigga surrenders, but I'm gon' fuck that bitch first." Then he hung up.

Tyck asked after the phone went dead in my ear, "Why you look like you done seen a ghost?"

I replied, "That was Echo, apparently, Marcus is still holding on to that white bitch we came across."

"So, what's he gonna do?" Tyck asked.

"He's gonna take her away from him."

***

"You gotta get rid of that baby. We ain't living right, and we ain't gonna keep something that them niggas can use as bait. So tomorrow, yo' ass is getting an abortion," Marcus said coldly, as if our child didn't mean anything to him.

"The hell I am. This is my body and my baby ain't getting sucked out of it. Fuck you, Marcus," I said to him with tears in my eyes.

"Fuck me? Nah, fuck you if you think I'ma let you bring a child into this world while I got a street beef going on. They almost got to you tonight. What you think they goin' to do if we bring a child into this world?"

"They didn't get me though. I did everything you taught me, Marcus. Look, I'm safe. I can keep our baby safe, too," I cried out and hoped he'd change his mind, but Marcus was a hard man to convince and once his mind was made up, it was a wrap.

"I'm taking you tomorrow to get an abortion and then I'm moving you to another location until this shit blows over. Now you can go up in that clinic willingly or with a foot in your ass," he demanded and then walked off leaving me with a broken heart.

***

"Yo, Feelow got a call from Echo last night talking 'bout kidnapping the white girl to make him surrender," I said as Trap and Creep looked at me confused.

Creep asked, "Man, what the fuck you talking, bout? What white girl?" I didn't know that Marcus had kept the girl a secret from his crew. I had only thought he just kept her at home, so she wouldn't be a product of the streets.

Trap stated, "Wait, wait, wait. Are you trying to tell us that Marcus has been hiding a white girl all this time from us and now somehow Echo has found out about her?"

"Yeah Trap, that's what I'm saying. Damn, I thought you niggas knew. Anyway, Echo is planning to swipe her ass and apparently, he made his first move, but his man let her slip away. Also, one of y'all boys got knocked. Apparently, he'd been arrested and Marcus sent the girl to pick him up when he got released. Somehow, Echo found out and had the girl followed, but homegirl was taught very well and slid away." I could tell by the look in their eyes that they hadn't heard about losing another team member yet.

Creep hopped out of his chair and lunged at me in anger, but Trap jumped up and stopped him right at the same time his cell phone rang. He answered and said, "Yeah, we ready." Then he hung up. He looked from Creep to me and said, "That was Marcus. He said C-John got clipped in the head last night and to get ready for a war."

***

I was jonesin for a hit when a black SUV with dark tinted windows pulled up in front of me. The window slowly slid down and there sat Toe Tag looking at me. He smiled and asked, "What's up with that good head, Carla? You feel like spending some time with a nigga?" I wasn't about to turn down his offer because it didn't seem like anything else was going to come through, plus he blessed me with plenty of dope last time, so I hopped in the passenger seat of his ride and he pulled off. This time he took me to a motel where it would be just me and him. I asked about his boys and he said, "Girl, I'm feeling a little greedy right now and want that pussy to myself tonight. You good with that?"

I shrugged my shoulders and said, "Sure. Whatever you like."

As soon as we walked into the motel room, he told me, "Go on in there, and wash that pussy up for me. I wanna see how it tastes this time. I'ma be here waiting on you with a hard dick when you get out, so hurry up and get it ready." He watched as I took off my clothes and asked, "You wanna hit before you go in there?"

I nodded and said, "Yeah, I could sure use one." He passed me a baggie full of dope and said, "You know if you got off this shit, you'd make a good woman for a nigga like me. I mean, I'm feeling you like that, but I can't have a bitch that's on the pipe."

I was flattered but ignored his comment and put a hit on my pipe. I felt kinda guilty smoking it in front of him now but pushed that feeling to the side quickly when the smoke filled my lungs. I held it in for a minute and once I exhaled, I got up and went to the bathroom, so I could clean up. While I bathed, thoughts of him entered my mind. He seemed like a good nigga, but I enjoyed smoking crack and knew that I wasn't ready to give it up just yet. Getting high was the only thing I had to look forward to.

I could faintly hear him talking to someone as the water cascaded down my skin. I decided to get out and left the water running, so I could eavesdrop on him. "Yeah, I know that dumb muthafucka let that white bitch slide right through his hands. I told yo' ass to let me get her." He paused to listen to the person on the other end of the line whom I assumed to be one of his partners, and then he started to talk again. "Well, that's just another soldier out of our way. I wonder how that nigga felt about C-John's murder. I wish I could have seen that nigga's head when it splattered all over the concrete. Aiight, I'll get my guns ready and if I see Marcus before you, I'ma have his body slumped and traced in white lines just in time for the evening news."

My heart skipped a beat, and I rushed to hop back in the shower. I jumped when I heard Toe Tag's voice as he entered the bathroom. "Yo, what's taking you so long, Shawty? A nigga ready to slide up in something wet." He pulled back the curtain and saw the blood as it ran down my legs and asked, "Damn, you on that womanly thing y'all be having? Uh, what the fuck y'all call it?"

I looked at him, nodded my head, and replied, "I'm sorry, it looks like I just started my period. Can you take a rain check?"

***

"Oh, Stone. That was so nice. It's been a long time since I've been able to enjoy a man's touch," I said after Stone and I made love for the first time. We had been seeing each other now for months and it had progressed into something more than I had expected.

"Yeah Delores, that was beautiful. I knew you were the perfect woman for me ever since day one. It's been a long time since I've been this happy. I never thought I'd be able to move on, but because of you, my heart is ready."

His words were so sincere and so sweet and were ones I'd longed to hear. It was a shame that we'd never be able to enjoy our future together. I knew that what I was doing was wrong, but I would do just about anything to get in my son's good graces, even if I had to serve him Stone on a silver platter.

"What's that noise?" Stone asked and sat up really quick.

I looked at him like he was crazy and said, "Bay, you hearing things. Now come here and give me some more of that good ole fashioned lovin." Instead, he pushed my hands away and pulled the sheets off of him. He then slid into a pair of pants and pulled his gun from out of the bedside drawer not knowing that I had emptied the bullets earlier while he was asleep. When he reached for the doorknob, he turned to me and held a finger over his lips telling me to remain silent, but before he could grip the knob completely, the door was kicked in.

***

Marcus moved me to a new location after he took me to get an abortion. The sadness in my heart was heavy and also made some of the love I had for him die. After the abortion, I couldn't help, but wonder if the child I had carried could have possibly been Brandon's. The one time he made love to me, he didn't use any protection, and the timeline would have been correct. When I found out I was pregnant, I wanted to tell him, but I knew the kind of drama it would have caused. I wasn't prepared for that, so I kept it to myself every time I made the trip. However, I told Marcus hoping that it would change things between us and it did, but not in the way I wanted.

The new place was small, but cozy, and I knew when he left me there that I would hardly see him. However, he popped up when it was time for a run and it would always end in an argument. "Are you gonna spend any time with me anymore, Marcus? I have needs too," I said, but he remained as cold as ever.

"I don't have time to stay up here and playhouse with you. Now if you just want some dick I'll break you off real quick, but I got shit going on in the streets, and I need to be there," he said in an agitated voice. Every time was a different excuse, so I finally just stopped asking. I knew that he was getting his dick wet, although, he denied it. But mark my words, one day I would catch his ass red handed.

***

I really didn't mean to cut myself as deep as I did, but it was a last-minute thought. When I overheard ToeTag on the phone, I knew that warning Marcus couldn't wait any longer, so I pressed as hard as I could with my nails and drew blood to make it appear as if I had started my period. I needed a reason for him to take me back where he got me from and I couldn't think of anything else.

"I'm sorry, Toe Tag. I'll make it up to you. Just come back in a few days and it should be off and then I'ma fuck you so good, you gonna wanna keep me forever," I said with a smile.

He pulled out a wad of cash out of his pocket, peeled off a couple of bills, and handed it to me and said, "I fucks with you, so I'ma hold you to your word. Don't let no one else get up in there before me, though." I hopped out of the SUV and when he pulled off, I went on a hunt for Marcus.

***

I fell backwards when the door hit me, but I bounced right back up. I couldn't believe my eyes when I noticed the person in front of me. "How the fuck?" I asked as Ditto stared back at me. I looked to make sure Delores was alright and noticed her getting dressed. Once she had on all her clothes, she proceeded to the door, but before she walked out, she turned to me and said, "I'm sorry, Stone. It was you or my son and no what, I'll always choose him."

Ditto laughed in my face when he walked out and then asked, "What did you think, Stone? Huh? You thought my mother was just letting you bang her because she wanted you? Huh? You big dumb muthafucka." He paused to see if I would respond, but I gave him silence, so he started to back up. "You did good, I must admit. You worked up under me for ten years, I never even had a clue, and then your bastard ass son joined in. What a coincidence. How long had you been planning my murder, Stone? Huh? How long did you sit up under me and plot to take my life? The whole ten years or was it a spur of the moment thing?"

I finally decided to speak and then cut my eyes to the gun that had flew out of my hand when he pushed the door in. "You don't deserve to be on this earth, Ditto, and I will…."

He cut me off when he noticed the gun and said, "Oh, that gun ain't gonna do you any good Stone, my mother emptied it when she put your ass to sleep," he said.

"You took the only woman that ever meant anything to me. You should have known that I'd come for you one day. Me and my son owed you." Then I lunged for him.

We tussled on the floor for a few minutes until the gun shot stopped us. Blood shot out of my thigh and I cringed at the pain. Ditto got up off of me and called Delores into the room and told her, "Bring me the duct tape, mother. I'ma torture this muthafucker before I stop him from breathing." Before Delores left the room, she picked up my gun off the floor and took it with her. Ditto said while he held his gun in my face, "Sit in that chair over there until she gets back. I'm about to make you feel my pain."

***

"Man, something don't feel right. It ain't like my pops to not answer his phone when I call," I said to Tray Pop, my new partner at the trap house since Montell was murdered.

"Yo Dawg, he prolly deep in a bitch guts right now. Shit, he enjoying that freedom since getting out of Ditto's grasp. Just chill and try him again in a couple of hours," Tray said and then passed me the blunt. I took a pull hoping it would calm my nerves, but it only enhanced my paranoia.

"Nah, I gotta go check on him. I'ma go check out the address he gave me for some chic he been bonin. You riding or you gon' chill?" I asked as I put my gun in the waist of my jeans.

"I'ma chill dawg just in case them fiends come through, but if you need me for anything, just holla and I got you," he stated and then leaned back in his chair to finish the blunt. I shook my head and walked out with the eerie feeling that my father was in deep shit.

***

"Oh my GOD, Feelow. Shit, I'm so glad to see you!" I said really loud, I'd noticed him and another nigga at the gas station around the corner from where Toe Tag dropped me off.

He asked, "What's up, Carla? You trying to spend some money?" I looked behind Feelow to the man in the car and got nervous because he wasn't familiar to me, but Feelow quickly eased my mind, "You good. Shit, that's my partner. He cool so what's up?"

I replied, "Feelow, I need to find Marcus. He's in trouble and I have to warn him before those niggas get to him."

He grabbed my arms to make me stay still and said, "Yo Carla, calm down. What the fuck you talkin about?"

I stopped my nervous jitter and said, "I've been tricking with a nigga called Toe Tag and his partners. They the ones that's been killing off ya'lls crew and they gon' make a move on Marcus next. I have to warn him."

I paused to take a breath and then blurted out, "Oh yeah, Toe Tag said something about a white girl too, but I didn't know what he was talking about."

Feelow turned around, opened his car door, and then turned back to me and said, "Get in. I'ma take you to Marcus so you can tell him everything you just told me." I jumped in his backseat, and when he got in, he looked at me in his rearview mirror. He drove off and for some reason I felt like Marcus would never get my message.

Chapter Twenty-Four

The address my father had given me was hard to find, but I finally located it. I felt in my gut that something was wrong because I continued to call his cell with no answer. I pulled up in the driveway and put my burner in my waistline before I turned my ride off and got out. I didn't even have a chance to ring the doorbell before an older lady opened the door. For some reason, the lady looked real familiar to me, but I was so worried about my pops that I couldn't place her. "Hi, how you doing, maam?" I asked and then pulled my pops photo up on my cell phone and asked, "I was wondering if you've seen this man anywhere around here?" Before she answered, my memory placed where I knew her from, but I didn't let on.

"Um, no, I'm sorry. I can't say that I have, but I wish I did because he sure is handsome," she replied in a flirtatious voice. I slowly put a hand on my gun and as soon as she blinked, I pulled it out and pointed it between her eyes.

"Don't say a muthafuckin word. If you do, I'ma split yo' wig in half. Do you understand me?" I said as I pushed her backwards with the tip of the gun.

Suddenly her whole demeanor changed and she began to cry, "I'm sorry. I'm so sorry. My son made me do it. He said he would kill me if I didn't seduce your father and lure him in."

"Ditto," I said, and then ordered her to step out of the house.

She asked, "Why are you making me come outside?"

I replied, "I'm just gonna put you somewhere safe until I take care of this and find my father." I then made her walk to the back of my car and popped the trunk open.

She begged, "Please don't put me in there. I'm claustrophobic. I'll suffocate. Please." I didn't give a fuck about shit she was saying, so I hit her over the head with the butt of my gun and pushed her in. I opened a small compartment that was hidden in there and pulled out a roll of black electrical tape and used it to secure her arms behind her back. I then taped up her ankles and her mouth to make sure she wasn't able to holler for help when she woke up. Once I had her secured, I shut the trunk quietly and went back to the front door. I crept back inside with the precision of a professional home invader and since the layout of the house wasn't familiar to me, I moved in slow motion from room to room and then I heard a sound.

***

I pulled up to the duplex I had rented out in another name just in case I needed it for a hide out. Tyck looked at me funny and then asked, "Yo, man. Who the fuck stays here?"

I smiled and looked in my rearview mirror and answered him, "I got this place a while back for situations like this."

He held a curious look in his eyes and asked his next question. "Situations like what? Nigga, stop speaking in code and just answer my damn question." Instead of answering him, I opened my door, got out, and then pushed my seat up so Carla could get out too.

"Come on, Carla. Marcus 'pose to meet us here when he get done handling his business." She looked up at me through frightened eyes but got out anyways. I then bent down and stuck my head in the car and said to Tyck, "You getting out nigga, or you gon' stay out here and miss all the fun." Tyck shook his head, got out, and slammed his door shut.

He walked around to where I was and said, "Man, I don't know what the fuck you about to do, but I don't think it's a good idea."

I laughed at his comment and replied, "Nigga, you just confused the fuck outta me."

We walked inside of the sparsely furnished duplex and I told Carla, "Go head and strip for a nigga. We gon' have a little fun until my boy shows up." She didn't budge. I pulled my burner from my waist and got in her face. I asked her, "Did you not hear what I just said to you? Take them muthafuckin clothes off before I rip that shit off."

She slowly began to undress and when she was completely naked, she asked, "How long will it be before Marcus gets here?"

I undid my pants, pulled my dick out, and then sat on the sofa. I looked at her as I stroked it and then answered her question, "I don't know, Carla. It depends on how good you suck my dick. Now come on over here and put them lips to good use." When she hesitated, I turned to Tyck and said, "Yo man, give this bitch something to smoke to get her started. Make it a big one, so she'll chill the fuck out."

Tyck pulled some dope out of his pocket and walked it over to her, but surprisingly she turned it down. I was curious, so I asked, "What's up, Carla? You suddenly don't smoke no more?"

She shook her head and replied, "Could you call Marcus and find out how long he's gonna be?" I stood up, walked back over to her, and grabbed her by the hair.

I said angrily, "Bitch, I'm running this shit so you need to stay in your place. Now get down on them knees and suck this muthafucka."

"Yo Fee, I got shit to do man, so I need to get outta here," Tyck blurted out and the shit threw me off. I motioned for him to walk over to me and when he did, I unzipped his pants. Carla noticed what I had did and pulled back with a look of confusion in her eyes.

I said to her, "Don't worry about what I'm doing. You just stay focused on what you doing." Then I pulled her head back to me. I could tell that Tyck was uncomfortable with what I had done, so I told him. "It's alright, Dawg. I'ma take this bitch in the back and handle my business. Just chill for a minute. I'll try not to take too long."

Tyck shook his head. "Man, you wildin' out," he said right before I took Carla in the bedroom.

***

I saw him when I walked into the sub shop and wished I had a phone, so I could call Feelow right then. I decided that I needed one for times like this. "Hey, Marcus. Long time no see," I said when I walked up to the counter beside him.

He turned to look at me when he heard his name and said, "What's up, Keish. You aiight?"

"Yeah. I just been chillin," I replied.

"You still mad at me?" he asked with a smile that made me wet. I did still feel some type of way about him dissin me the last time we were together, but him standing in front of me made me soften up and push it to the side.

I shook my head and stated, "Nah. I been forgot about that. We good."

His order came up on the counter and after he paid for it, he turned to me and asked, "What you out here getting into?" He looked around the small shop. Then added, "Where ya boy at?"

I ignored that question but answered the other one. "I was just coming to get something to eat. I don't know if you heard or not, but I done got knocked up," I said to see how he would respond.

"Oh, yeah? Damn, no wonder yo shit thickening up. Is it true that pregnant pussy the best?" he asked with raised eyebrows.

I blushed a little because Marcus always had that effect on me when he was in my presence. I stated, "There's only one way to find out."

He then looked me up and down and asked, "You wanna chill with me for a couple of hours? I could use a little something wet on this dick, and I ain't met a bitch yet that could ride one like you."

Thoughts of eating instantly left my mind, although, my stomach growled with anticipation. It was a shame that me and Feelow were on the outs because I was down for a threesome. This would have been the perfect opportunity for Fee to go through with his plan, but because of his stubbornness, he would miss out. I said to Marcus with a smile, "Lead the way, Daddy."

***

I made my way to the door. I'd heard a noise behind and slowly opened it, only to find the room empty. When I turned around to go try another door, I heard the noise again. I turned and went back in the room with my gun still pointed out in front of me. I checked the closet first but found nothing. I walked into the bathroom and didn't see anything unusual, but before I turned around, I noticed the trail of blood. I reached out to pull the shower curtain open and almost lost my breath.

"Oh my God, Pops. Hold on. I got you," I cried out when I found him nodding in and out of consciousness. His wrists were bound and his mouth was covered with duct tape. "Damn, Damn, Damn." I pulled out my cell phone, called Tray Pop, and said, 'Yo man, I found my pops, but he ain't in good shape. Get a hold of Marcus and let him know we'll be at the hospital. I'll call as soon as he can tell me who did this to him, but I got a feeling that I already know." I untied my father and used all my strength to pull him out of the car and then I drove like a bat out of hell to get him some help, forgetting all about the woman in my trunk.

***

"Suck on them nuts like they some grapes, Keisha. Shit girl, you always know what you doin," I said in pleasure as I rotated my hips to the rhythm of Keisha's head. I heard my phone buzz but was too lost in the thrones of passion to answer. Keisha dropped my nut sack from her jaws and licked around my asshole before coming up for air. She stood on her knees and played in her pussy while she pulled one of her fat nipples between her lips. "Come on up here and sit on yo master," I said while I held my dick in my hand. She got up and squatted over my manhood. As soon as the head disappeared inside of her, my phone buzzed again.

I decided to ignore it once again, thinking that it may have just been Krystal calling to nag me. She seemed to have a radar that always made her call me when I was deep in some pussy. Ever since I made her get that abortion, she'd been extra needy. I didn't even want to give her the dick that much anymore because she needed to learn how to stay in her place. "Ah, shit. Yeah Keish, that shit about pregnant pussy is true. That shit wet as fuck," I said as I laid back and watched her pussy swallow me. She put her palms down flat on my chest and worked her hips like a professional pole dancer, right when my phone buzzed again.

I went ahead and picked it up just to see who it was fucking up my flow and saw Tray Pop's number. I answered and said, "Nigga, this shit better be good as the pussy I'm in."

I then listened to what he said, "Yo Marcus, Paris is on his way taking his pops to the hospital. He said he pretty bad off, dawg."

I pushed Keisha back and when she fell off of me she left traces of pussy juice behind. "What the fuck you just say?" I asked more alert of the conversation.

"Man, Paris couldn't reach Stone, so he went to check out an address that he'd given him and when he got there, Ditto's momma answered the door. He locked that bitch in his trunk and then went in to see what else he could find and found his pops leaking in the bathtub," Tray Pop stated all in one breath.

"Damn. I'ma wrap up here, but call me if you hear anything else," I said and hung up.

Keisha caressed my shoulder like we were a real couple and asked, "Is everything okay, Marcus?"

I turned my head and looked at her like she'd done something wrong and said, "Nah, come on and finish me up, so I can get outta here."

She smacked her lips and said, "Damn Marcus, you so disrespectful to me and I don't even understand why."

I laid back with my dick still at attention and said, "Yeah. I'm sure my boy Feelow would say the same shit about you."

***

I heard the car when it pulled up and hurriedly finished my task. I then climbed out the window and left the bitch to fend for herself. She actually thought that by saving my life, I would forgive her for taking my father, but I would never forgive her for that. I'd slit my own throat first, I wasn't sure if Stone was still breathing when I left or not, but I couldn't spare any minutes to stick around and find out. However, it would be hard to believe that he could live through what I'd just put him through.

I pulled my phone out of my pocket and dialed his number. "Yeah, speak to me," he said when he answered.

"I need a place to hide out for a minute. Can you hook me up?" I asked the man on the other end of the line.

"Did you handle what you needed to handle?" he asked.

Since I wasn't sure of Stone's outcome, I didn't want to answer the question, but I also didn't have a choice. "I'm halfway there, but I ran into a small bump in the road and almost didn't make it out. I need to chill for a minute, and then I'll come back full force," I stated.

"Aiight, but when you go back in, I'ma send some people with you since you can't seem to handle it by yourself." Then he hung up.

***

I had been sitting in the living room for over an hour waiting for Feelow to get done with Carla. I decided to make a call to Marcus to let him know what was going on, but his phone kept going to voicemail. I found that odd because he always kept his phone on. I then called Trap."Yo Man, what's good?" he asked over the loud music I heard being played in the background.

"Aye man, what's going on there? Sounds like y'all having a party and shit," I stated.

"Man, we decided to call over a few homies and get a little show going. We got some fat asses bouncing up in this bitch. You should come over, nigga and enjoy yourself!" Trap shouted.

I was shocked at how relaxed Marcus' crew was, even though they had been getting dropped on every corner. I knew that life still had to go on, so I kept my thoughts about it to myself. "Nah, man. I'm good where I'm at. Fee in the back room blowing Carla's back out and shit. That nigga been in there for over an hour, dawg. Bitch ain't gonna have no pussy bottom when he get through," I said and shared a laugh with Trap.

He then had me reminiscing on the old days. "Man, they say Carla used to be that bitch back in the day, but then she got on that pipe and it turned her whole world upside down. I sho' wish I'd known her back then." He paused for a second and then stated, "Man, I know you done had a piece of that pussy. Nigga, tell me how it was."

Trap and Creep didn't know that I preferred men over women and although I wasn't ashamed of it, I didn't want to disappoint them, so I let them believe whatever they wanted. Somehow, although, I was around the same age as Trap he looked up to me like I was his idol. I had only known him for a short period of time, but for some reason, I didn't want to let him down or stain his image of me. I tried to keep it as real as I could with him and told him half of the truth. "Man, you know I went away at fifteen years old for six years, so I never had the chance to tap that ass, but you know she used to be called 'Cum For Me Carla' cause that bitch was the finest thang walking. I'd heard about her hitting the pipe when I was still in the joint, and by the time I got out, that bitch was strung out.

Trap sounded disappointed when he said, "Damn, man. I hate that you missed out on all those years, but at least you made it out while you're still young and can enjoy life."

He stopped talking and hollered something to someone in the background and then came back on the line and said, "Well man, if you change your mind, there's plenty over here for you."

"Aiight Trap, I'll keep that in mind. Peace." Then I hung up. I got tired of waiting on Feelow's ass and went into the room to see what was taking him so long. When I opened the door and walked in, I wasn't prepared for what I walked in on.

***

I heard him moan and shot up out of the chair I'd fallen asleep in and went to check on him. "Pops. Pops, it's me. I'm right here," I said and then pushed the button for the nurse to be alerted. His eyes opened and he looked around the room before he settled his eyes on me. He tried to speak but broke out into a coughing fit instead. I panicked and pushed the call button again. No sooner than I let go, a nurse burst into the room and rushed by his side. I moved out of the way, so she could get to him. I watched as she prepared him a glass of water and then held it to his lips so he could drink.

His coughing ceased and then the nurse turned to me and said, "He's okay. His throat was just dry from all the tubes he's had stuck down it, but he should be good now." Her smile was warm and welcoming and her eyes seemed to light up the whole room.

I walked over to the bed beside her and said, "Thanks. My name is Paris."

She giggled and asked, "Paris as in France? Is that your real name or something the streets gave you?"

I replied in a soft voice, "Nah, my name is Stanley Parrish Jr., but my pops here, started calling me Paris when I was old enough to piss by myself. What's your name?"

"I'm Torrie, short for Victoria and it's very nice to meet you Stanley Parrish Jr.," she shyly said and then continued. "Well, I have to finish my rounds before clock out time, so I'll leave you two alone. Have a good night."

Before she walked out, I stopped her and asked, "How's the food in this place because my ass is hungry as hell."

She giggled again and said, "Well, I don't know how hungry hell is, but the food here is edible. I'm actually going to stop by there and grab a bite before I go home. You're more than welcome to join me."

I looked at my father who moaned and then turned one side of his mouth up as if he were trying to smile and then turned back to her and said, "Just tell me when and I'll meet you there."

***

"Hold up, Keisha. I gotta take a piss," I said before I got up to go to the bathroom. When I came back in the room, Keisha was getting dressed so I asked, "Damn, what's gotten into you? I usually gotta kick yo ass out or leave you hanging."

Her answer surprised me. "I'm trying to change my ways, Marcus. Ya know, now that I got a baby on the way."

I asked her because I wanted to know, "Is Feelow the daddy?"

She answered me with tear filled eyes, "I honestly don't know, Marcus. I done fucked and sucked so many different niggas that I can't even tell you. When I told him, he cussed me the hell out and told me that I need to find the real daddy and have him take care of it. I ain't seen or talked to him since."

For some strange reason I honestly felt bad for her. "Are you gonna keep it?" I asked and then she snapped on me.

"What kind of question is that? I know I ain't nothing, but a trick to these niggas around here, but I do got a heart. Marcus, there's no way I can kill this baby. Not even if I have to raise it alone. I just gotta figure out how."

I sighed heavily and stated, "Look Keisha, I fuck with you even though I know yo ass was plotting with my boy to take me out, but I don't hold that shit against you. I blame his ass because he was supposed to be my brotha and then shit changed." I stopped talking and got in my thoughts for a minute and then said, "I mean, me and him cool for now, but I know that nigga a dog when it comes to women and because he on some other shit. I'ma step-up and help just because you being sincere and there's a chance the baby could be his. I want you to stay here for the rest of the night and tomorrow before check out time, I'ma come scoop you and help you find a place to rest your head."

A tear fell from her eyes and then she jumped up, wrapped her arms around my neck, and said, "Thank you, Marcus. Thank you, but how am I going to keep my bills up? I can't suck dick forever."

I smiled at her comment and said, "I got you, but you can't be letting all types of niggas up in the place. I'll set you up with a job that you can do on the inside and under no circumstances ever let Feelow know where you stay." She agreed with what I'd said, and before I left her, I stated, "Keisha, if you stab me in the back after I do this for you, I'll kill you and that bastard you carrying. I give you my word on that." Then I walked out.

***

When I walked in the room, Feelow had Carla on the bed doggie style with his hand in her hair gripping it tightly. I watched as he rammed into her with all his strength and then noticed the knife in his other hand. I listened in shock. "So, yo' ass wanna save Marcus, huh? All you fucking whores wanna run y'all dumb asses around here behind him when he really don't give a fuck about y'all."

"Please, Feelow. Please. I won't say anything. Please just let me go," she cried out as tears streamed heavily down her face.

I spoke up and tried to break Feelow out of his wrath, "Yo Fee, nigga what the fuck you doing? Man, put that knife down and let the girl go."

He turned his head and looked at me with an evil in his eyes I hadn't seen before and said, "Aye Tyck, my nigga, you gonna wanna stay and watch this shit. Its 'bout to be some real live shit in this bitch." Feelow then positioned the knife at Carla's asshole and before I could stop him, he slid it in, its sharp edge sliced her open even more.

"Ahh. Ahh, somebody help me!" she screamed and tried to pull from his hold on her, but his strength outweighed hers. When he pulled the knife out. It was covered in blood and feces.

I made one final attempt to save her. "Feelow man, that's enough, she gets the message. Now let her go."

Feelow continued to ignore my pleas. Since he wasn't paying me no attention, I pulled my cell phone out and started to record him. He started up on Carla again and said, "Bitch, you should have stayed with that nigga Toe Tag instead of trying to save Marcus, cause he gon' get his one way or another." He put the knife to Carla's neck and pumped in faster, and as soon as he came, he slid the blade across her throat and silenced her cries forever.

Three Months Later…

I was finally released from the hospital and was relieved to be home. Although, Ditto had fucked me up something good had come from my ordeal, Paris had finally found love. I was happy for him because Torrie was a nice girl and also a square in the streets. She reminded me a lot of his momma and that scared me more than anything did. "You ready, Pops?" Paris asked as he walked up behind me.

"Yeah son, let's knock this out so I can get out of this damn chair. Whoo, I can't fuckin wait," I said right before Torrie walked in the room. We had all found a nice home to live in away from the streets that we sold dope on. Torrie was also seven weeks pregnant with my first grandchild, and I had never seen my son happier. I was still disappointed that Delores had did me dirty, but I didn't have to worry about her anymore. Once Paris and I decided to let her go, she committed suicide by jumping in front of a semi-truck. She knew as well as we did that Ditto was still out there, lurking, and I guessed she didn't want to face him or beg for his forgiveness anymore. So, instead of waiting for him to come back and take her life, she took herself out.

Torrie said, "Yeah, you need to have them legs strong enough to push this grandson of yours around." She rubbed her growing stomach and smiled at me.

Paris said, "Yeah Pops, we gon' pimp that stroller out with twenty twos on chrome."

We all shared a laugh and then Paris added, "My son gon be pimping at birth." Torrie punched him in the arm and then tiptoed to reach his lips and kissed them gently and stated, "I gotta get to work, but I'll be home in time to cook dinner. I love y'all and I'll see you later." Then she bent down and kissed my cheek. We all walked out of the house together but got in separate vehicles. Torrie had to run back in the house because she had forgotten something. Paris went ahead and pulled out of the driveway and when he saw her come back out he began to pull off. Torrie got in her car and turned the key in the ignition right before it burst into flames.

***

My heart broke for Paris and I could feel his pain deeply. He had finally found love and was gonna be a dad, and it was all taken from him at the turn of a switch. That was why I never wanted Krystal to be out in the streets, riding alongside of me. Niggas in the game had to learn to separate home from work and although, I used her to make my runs to Baltimore, I never went with her so that way we couldn't be linked together.

"Marcus, what you thinking about?" Krystal asked and then snuggled up closer to me. I hadn't been the best man to her and still, she stuck by my side like a true rider.

I looked at her and put my arm around her and said, "I was thinking about how I could of easily been Torrie. That's why you gotta understand that I can't rest my head here with you permanently. Ditto's still out there somewhere and that nigga Echo. I also never know when Feelow's gonna switch up because he goes back and forth." I took a breath and then continued, "I know you want me in the bed with you and one day that time will come, but for now, I just need you to hold me down."

"Marcus, I got you and I do understand, but it gets lonely here by myself all the time. I know you out there romancing other women too, and that shit weighs heavy on my mind," she said, breaking my chill mood.

"Look, until you have proof or catch me in anotha bitch's guts, shut the fuck up about it. You always coming with that shit fucking up the mood. I gotta go," I stated angrily and then got up to grab my keys.

"The truck is packed up for B-Line, so I need you to make that happen this weekend. Call me when you make it back," I said and then walked out slamming the door behind me.

***

"Man, you can say what you wanna say, but you ain't smart enough to catch that nigga slippin," Swag T said through bloodshot eyes, but I wasn't listening to shit she was saying.

"I was really feeling that bitch, man. When I get my hands on Marcus, I'ma shove a blade up that nigga ass the same way he did Carla," I said through clenched teeth. I had went back to look for her a few days after dropping her off, but no one had seen her around. I was disappointed but refused to give up.

Feelow ended up calling and telling me about Marcus hooking up with her, and then described the gory details of what he did to her precious body. That shit had broken my heart. I had planned to pull her off the streets and off that shit and hopefully make an honest woman out of her. I should have never let her get out of my truck that day and although, some time had passed, I still hadn't gotten over it. Somehow, I would find Marcus and figure out where he hid his little white bitch, and then I'd make her feel the same way Carla must have felt when the blade slid across her jugular vein.

***

"So, you telling me that Fee got that nigga thinking that Marcus took out Carla ass?" Trap asked me as we sat there and waited for Marcus to show.

"Yeah man, but he don't know I recorded it and if he finds out he gon be pissed and come at me too," I said just as Marcus walked in the house where we were at. Me and Trap eyed each other and then got up to give Marcus dap.

He then sat down and asked, "What the fuck was so important? You niggas acting like y'all done hit that shit. Acting all funny and stuff."

I pulled out my phone and showed him the clip of Feelow with Carla. "Man, what the fuck is that?" he asked.

I replied, "Man, I'm showing you this because Feelow got Toe Tag thinking this was your work. That nigga been acting erratic and shit lately, dawg. Toe Tag's pissed because he was feeling this bitch."

"Man, I don't understand. What made him do that shit?" Marcus inquired.

I told him the truth, "Me and Fee was at the store and Carla ran up talking bout warning you that Echo and his boys was gonna try and hit you and that it was them taking out all your boys. Feelow made her think he was gonna take her to you so she could warn you, but he did this to her instead and then reported it to Toe Tag."

Marcus stood in anger and said, "I just don't understand what changed him to be like this. I want to blame shit on Ditto, but he's gotten worse."

I said, "Yo Marcus, I was in prison with a nigga who got a hold of some bad shit and it made him act the same way Feelow's acting." I noticed the look on Trap's face and remembered that he wasn't aware of Feelow's habit, and I didn't feel like explaining it to him. I continued with my story. "Anyway, dude smoked some shit that had been laced with rat poison and ended up dying. I was there when he smoked that shit Echo gave him and I'm sure that's what he's still putting in his pipe. He's only gonna get worse."

Trap looked surprised, but asked the ultimate question, "So how do we get him off that shit and help him?"

I looked at Marcus for the answer and he didn't disappoint. "We kill him."

***

The bus ride to the prison was long and loud but gave me time to think about what I'd done. I continued to tell myself that Marcus would come around, but in my heart, I knew that I was in this alone and would never see him again.

When the bus pulled into the prison, I looked out the caged window at the length of the razor wire that lined the prison fences and asked myself, "What have I done?" I felt a tear drop from my eye, and then stepped off the bus to face my new reality.

There were several guards lined up along the walkway and I could have sworn that I heard them all saying the same thing and although, their mouths weren't moving I could hear them as they chanted.

"Dumb Bitch."

"Hey, the dumb bitch has finally made it."

"Ha Ha Ha. You dumb ass bitch."

"That muthafucka got a new bitch now."

Their laughs filled my mind and wouldn't stop. All I wanted was for them to be quiet, but they got louder and louder instead. The handcuffs that were around my wrists were attached to a belly chain and made it to where I couldn't even cover my ears.

"Hey, y'all, Look. It's that dumb bitch."

"Dumb bitch. Dumb bitch. Dumb bitch."

Everything around me started to spin and I felt as if I could no longer stand. My feet became heavier with every step, but I managed to make it to the end of the sidewalk and to the door.

It buzzed open as soon as I got to it and when I walked in, I could have sworn that I saw Marcus in front of me. I cried out, "Marcus! Marcus, save me. Please." But he just stood there and stared at me then he started to laugh with the rest of them. I continued to walk closer to him, but the closer I got, the further away he became.

All of a sudden, he disappeared and when I took another step, I passed out.

Chapter Twenty-Five

Every time I made the trip to Baltimore, I told myself that it would be the last one, but I knew that it was a lie. I enjoyed getting away from everything, but was the chance I was taking worth it?

Brandon tried to convince me to leave Marcus and stay with him every time I went, but I couldn't. I felt like I still owed Marcus for saving my life all those months ago, plus, my love for him was deep.

Marcus' visits to see me were getting less frequent and I felt in my gut that he had someone else taking my place. I tried and tried to get him to admit it, but what man in their right mind would?

Brandon suggested that I start pocketing some of the money and stash it just in case I came across an emergency or if Marcus left me for dead, but I refused to take anything from him without him knowing it. I wasn't that kind of person. When I got back to town, I decided not to go back where Marcus had moved me to. Instead, I went back to the place we once shared and when I didn't see his vehicle there, I got out and let myself in.

I walked all over the house just to see if I could find traces of another woman, and it caused my heart to ease when I didn't find anything. However, I still had a feeling in my gut and I didn't like it. I went into our bedroom and ran my hands over the bed we used to share. The covers were still as soft as ever. The same ones that covered such a hardened man with no heart.

I pulled out the drawer of the bedside table and saw the gun. I hurriedly shut it and opened it right back up. I pulled the gun out and sat there in deep thought for a minute before putting the weapon in my purse.

I got up and left the room, leaving only my scent behind. I was on another mission and my determination caused me to walk fast, making my breath heavy. I got in my ride and drove all the streets of the city until I finally found it.

He had it parked right there in front of the room as if he had no shame. Before I let my presence be known, I listened just to make sure I was at the right one. The moans coming from inside were loud and clear, and I knew that whoever was in there didn't plan on being disturbed.

I changed my mind all of a sudden and started to walk away, but then I heard another voice and stopped in my tracks. I turned back, knowing that this was my moment and I would not let it slip away. I couldn't because it would eat away at me forever. I had come too far to back out now.

I put my hand on the doorknob and was shocked to find it unlocked. My small hand gripped it tightly as I pushed the door open slowly in hopes of finding what I'd been looking for.

To Be Continued…
Protégé of a Legend 2
Coming Soon

Lock Down Publications and Ca$h Presents assisted publishing packages.

BASIC PACKAGE $499
Editing
Cover Design
Formatting

UPGRADED PACKAGE $800
Typing
Editing
Cover Design
Formatting

ADVANCE PACKAGE $1,200
Typing
Editing
Cover Design
Formatting
Copyright registration
Proofreading
Upload book to Amazon

LDP SUPREME PACKAGE $1,500
Typing
Editing
Cover Design
Formatting
Copyright registration
Proofreading
Set up Amazon account
Upload book to Amazon
Advertise on LDP Amazon and Facebook page

***Other services available upon request. Additional charges may apply

Lock Down Publications
P.O. Box 944
Stockbridge, GA 30281-9998
Phone # 470 303-9761

Submission Guideline

Submit the first three chapters of your completed manuscript to ldpsubmissions@gmail.com, subject line: Your book's title. The manuscript must be in a .doc file and sent as an attachment. Document should be in Times New Roman, double spaced and in size 12 font. Also, provide your synopsis and full contact information. If sending multiple submissions, they must each be in a separate email.

Have a story but no way to send it electronically? You can still submit to LDP/Ca$h Presents. Send in the first three chapters, written or typed, of your completed manuscript to:

LDP: Submissions Dept
Po Box 944
Stockbridge, Ga 30281

DO NOT send original manuscript. Must be a duplicate.

Provide your synopsis and a cover letter containing your full contact information.

Thanks for considering LDP and Ca$h Presents.

NEW RELEASES

THE BRICK MAN 4 by KING RIO
HOOD CONSIGLIERE by KEESE
PRETTY GIRLS DO NASTY THINGS by NICOLE GOOSBY
PROTÉGÉ OF A LEGEND by COREY ROBINSON

Coming Soon from Lock Down Publications/Ca$h Presents

BLOOD OF A BOSS **VI**

SHADOWS OF THE GAME II

TRAP BASTARD II

By **Askari**

LOYAL TO THE GAME **IV**

By **T.J. & Jelissa**

IF TRUE SAVAGE **VIII**

MIDNIGHT CARTEL IV

DOPE BOY MAGIC IV

CITY OF KINGZ III

NIGHTMARE ON SILENT AVE II

THE PLUG OF LIL MEXICO II

By **Chris Green**

BLAST FOR ME **III**

A SAVAGE DOPEBOY III

CUTTHROAT MAFIA III

DUFFLE BAG CARTEL VII

HEARTLESS GOON VI

By **Ghost**

A HUSTLER'S DECEIT III

KILL ZONE II

BAE BELONGS TO ME III

By **Aryanna**

KING OF THE TRAP III

By **T.J. Edwards**

GORILLAZ IN THE BAY V

3X KRAZY III

STRAIGHT BEAST MODE II

De'Kari

KINGPIN KILLAZ IV

STREET KINGS III

PAID IN BLOOD III

CARTEL KILLAZ IV

DOPE GODS III

Hood Rich

SINS OF A HUSTLA II

ASAD

RICH $AVAGE II

By Martell Troublesome Bolden

YAYO V

Bred In The Game 2

S. Allen

CREAM III

THE STREETS WILL TALK II

By Yolanda Moore

SON OF A DOPE FIEND III

HEAVEN GOT A GHETTO II

By Renta

LOYALTY AIN'T PROMISED III

By Keith Williams

I'M NOTHING WITHOUT HIS LOVE II

SINS OF A THUG II

TO THE THUG I LOVED BEFORE II

IN A HUSTLER I TRUST II

By Monet Dragun

QUIET MONEY IV

EXTENDED CLIP III

THUG LIFE IV

By **Trai'Quan**

THE STREETS MADE ME IV

By **Larry D. Wright**

IF YOU CROSS ME ONCE II

By **Anthony Fields**

THE STREETS WILL NEVER CLOSE IV

By K'ajji

HARD AND RUTHLESS III

KILLA KOUNTY III

By Khufu

MONEY GAME III

By Smoove Dolla

JACK BOYS VS DOPE BOYS II

A GANGSTA'S QUR'AN V

COKE GIRLZ II

By Romell Tukes

MURDA WAS THE CASE II

Elijah R. Freeman

THE STREETS NEVER LET GO II

By Robert Baptiste

AN UNFORESEEN LOVE III

By **Meesha**

KING OF THE TRENCHES III
by **GHOST & TRANAY ADAMS**

MONEY MAFIA II

LOYAL TO THE SOIL III

By **Jibril Williams**

QUEEN OF THE ZOO II

By **Black Migo**

VICIOUS LOYALTY III

By Kingpen

A GANGSTA'S PAIN III

By J-Blunt

CONFESSIONS OF A JACKBOY III

By Nicholas Lock

GRIMEY WAYS II

By Ray Vinci

KING KILLA II

By Vincent "Vitto" Holloway

BETRAYAL OF A THUG II

By Fre$h

THE MURDER QUEENS II

By Michael Gallon

THE BIRTH OF A GANGSTER II

By Delmont Player

TREAL LOVE II

By Le'Monica Jackson

FOR THE LOVE OF BLOOD II

By Jamel Mitchell

RAN OFF ON DA PLUG II

By Paper Boi Rari

HOOD CONSIGLIERE II

By Keese

PRETTY GIRLS DO NASTY THINGS II

By Nicole Goosby

PROTÉGÉ OF A LEGEND II

By Corey Robinson

Available Now

RESTRAINING ORDER **I & II**

By **CA$H & Coffee**

LOVE KNOWS NO BOUNDARIES **I II & III**

By **Coffee**

RAISED AS A GOON I, II, III & IV

BRED BY THE SLUMS I, II, III

BLAST FOR ME I & II

ROTTEN TO THE CORE I II III

A BRONX TALE I, II, III

DUFFLE BAG CARTEL I II III IV V VI

HEARTLESS GOON I II III IV V

A SAVAGE DOPEBOY I II

DRUG LORDS I II III

CUTTHROAT MAFIA I II

KING OF THE TRENCHES

By **Ghost**

LAY IT DOWN **I & II**

LAST OF A DYING BREED I II

BLOOD STAINS OF A SHOTTA I & II III

By **Jamaica**

LOYAL TO THE GAME I II III

LIFE OF SIN I, II III

By **TJ & Jelissa**

BLOODY COMMAS I & II

SKI MASK CARTEL I II & III

KING OF NEW YORK I II,III IV V

RISE TO POWER I II III

COKE KINGS I II III IV V

BORN HEARTLESS I II III IV

KING OF THE TRAP I II

By **T.J. Edwards**

IF LOVING HIM IS WRONG…I & II

LOVE ME EVEN WHEN IT HURTS I II III

By **Jelissa**

WHEN THE STREETS CLAP BACK I & II III

THE HEART OF A SAVAGE I II III

MONEY MAFIA

LOYAL TO THE SOIL I II

By **Jibril Williams**

A DISTINGUISHED THUG STOLE MY HEART I II & III

LOVE SHOULDN'T HURT I II III IV

RENEGADE BOYS I II III IV

PAID IN KARMA I II III

SAVAGE STORMS I II III

AN UNFORESEEN LOVE I II

By **Meesha**

A GANGSTER'S CODE I &, II III

A GANGSTER'S SYN I II III

THE SAVAGE LIFE I II III

CHAINED TO THE STREETS I II III

BLOOD ON THE MONEY I II III

A GANGSTA'S PAIN I II

By J-Blunt

PUSH IT TO THE LIMIT

By **Bre' Hayes**

BLOOD OF A BOSS **I, II, III, IV, V**

SHADOWS OF THE GAME

TRAP BASTARD

By **Askari**

THE STREETS BLEED MURDER **I, II & III**

THE HEART OF A GANGSTA I II& III

By **Jerry Jackson**

CUM FOR ME I II III IV V VI VII VIII

An **LDP Erotica Collaboration**

BRIDE OF A HUSTLA **I II & II**

THE FETTI GIRLS **I, II& III**

CORRUPTED BY A GANGSTA I, II III, IV

BLINDED BY HIS LOVE

THE PRICE YOU PAY FOR LOVE I, II ,III

DOPE GIRL MAGIC I II III

By **Destiny Skai**

WHEN A GOOD GIRL GOES BAD

By **Adrienne**

THE COST OF LOYALTY I II III

By Kweli

A GANGSTER'S REVENGE **I II III & IV**

THE BOSS MAN'S DAUGHTERS I II III IV V

A SAVAGE LOVE **I & II**

BAE BELONGS TO ME I II

A HUSTLER'S DECEIT I, II, III

WHAT BAD BITCHES DO I, II, III

SOUL OF A MONSTER I II III

KILL ZONE

A DOPE BOY'S QUEEN I II III

By **Aryanna**

A KINGPIN'S AMBITON

A KINGPIN'S AMBITION **II**

I MURDER FOR THE DOUGH

By **Ambitious**

TRUE SAVAGE I II III IV V VI VII

DOPE BOY MAGIC I, II, III

MIDNIGHT CARTEL I II III

CITY OF KINGZ I II

NIGHTMARE ON SILENT AVE

THE PLUG OF LIL MEXICO II

By **Chris Green**

A DOPEBOY'S PRAYER

By **Eddie "Wolf" Lee**

THE KING CARTEL **I, II & III**

By **Frank Gresham**

THESE NIGGAS AIN'T LOYAL **I, II & III**

By **Nikki Tee**

GANGSTA SHYT **I II &III**

By **CATO**

THE ULTIMATE BETRAYAL

By **Phoenix**

BOSS'N UP **I , II & III**

By **Royal Nicole**

I LOVE YOU TO DEATH

By **Destiny J**

I RIDE FOR MY HITTA

I STILL RIDE FOR MY HITTA

By **Misty Holt**

LOVE & CHASIN' PAPER

By **Qay Crockett**

TO DIE IN VAIN

SINS OF A HUSTLA

By **ASAD**

BROOKLYN HUSTLAZ

By **Boogsy Morina**

BROOKLYN ON LOCK I & II

By **Sonovia**

GANGSTA CITY

By **Teddy Duke**

A DRUG KING AND HIS DIAMOND I & II III

A DOPEMAN'S RICHES

HER MAN, MINE'S TOO I, II

CASH MONEY HO'S

THE WIFEY I USED TO BE I II

PRETTY GIRLS DO NASTY THINGS

By Nicole Goosby

TRAPHOUSE KING **I II & III**

KINGPIN KILLAZ I II III

STREET KINGS I II

PAID IN BLOOD **I II**

CARTEL KILLAZ I II III

DOPE GODS I II

By **Hood Rich**

LIPSTICK KILLAH **I, II, III**

CRIME OF PASSION I II & III

FRIEND OR FOE I II III

By **Mimi**

STEADY MOBBN' **I, II, III**

THE STREETS STAINED MY SOUL I II III

By **Marcellus Allen**

WHO SHOT YA **I, II, III**

SON OF A DOPE FIEND I II

HEAVEN GOT A GHETTO

Renta

GORILLAZ IN THE BAY **I II III IV**

TEARS OF A GANGSTA I II

3X KRAZY I II

STRAIGHT BEAST MODE

DE'KARI

TRIGGADALE I II III

MURDAROBER WAS THE CASE

Elijah R. Freeman

GOD BLESS THE TRAPPERS I, II, III

THESE SCANDALOUS STREETS I, II, III

FEAR MY GANGSTA I, II, III IV, V

THESE STREETS DON'T LOVE NOBODY I, II

BURY ME A G I, II, III, IV, V

A GANGSTA'S EMPIRE I, II, III, IV

THE DOPEMAN'S BODYGAURD I II

THE REALEST KILLAZ I II III

THE LAST OF THE OGS I II III

Tranay Adams

THE STREETS ARE CALLING

Duquie Wilson

MARRIED TO A BOSS I II III

By Destiny Skai & Chris Green

KINGZ OF THE GAME I II III IV V VI

Playa Ray

SLAUGHTER GANG I II III

RUTHLESS HEART I II III

By Willie Slaughter

FUK SHYT

By Blakk Diamond

DON'T F#CK WITH MY HEART I II

By Linnea

ADDICTED TO THE DRAMA I II III

IN THE ARM OF HIS BOSS II

By Jamila

YAYO I II III IV

A SHOOTER'S AMBITION I II

BRED IN THE GAME

By S. Allen

TRAP GOD I II III

RICH $AVAGE

MONEY IN THE GRAVE I II III

By Martell Troublesome Bolden

FOREVER GANGSTA

GLOCKS ON SATIN SHEETS I II

By Adrian Dulan

TOE TAGZ I II III IV

LEVELS TO THIS SHYT I II

By Ah'Million

KINGPIN DREAMS I II III

RAN OFF ON DA PLUG

By Paper Boi Rari

CONFESSIONS OF A GANGSTA I II III IV

CONFESSIONS OF A JACKBOY I II

By Nicholas Lock

I'M NOTHING WITHOUT HIS LOVE

SINS OF A THUG

TO THE THUG I LOVED BEFORE

A GANGSTA SAVED XMAS

IN A HUSTLER I TRUST

By Monet Dragun

CAUGHT UP IN THE LIFE I II III

THE STREETS NEVER LET GO

By Robert Baptiste

NEW TO THE GAME I II III

MONEY, MURDER & MEMORIES I II III

By **Malik D. Rice**

LIFE OF A SAVAGE I II III

A GANGSTA'S QUR'AN I II III IV

MURDA SEASON I II III

GANGLAND CARTEL I II III

CHI'RAQ GANGSTAS I II III

KILLERS ON ELM STREET I II III

JACK BOYZ N DA BRONX I II III

A DOPEBOY'S DREAM I II III

JACK BOYS VS DOPE BOYS

COKE GIRLZ

By Romell Tukes

LOYALTY AIN'T PROMISED I II

By Keith Williams

QUIET MONEY I II III

THUG LIFE I II III

EXTENDED CLIP I II

By **Trai'Quan**

THE STREETS MADE ME I II III

By **Larry D. Wright**

THE ULTIMATE SACRIFICE I, II, III, IV, V, VI

KHADIFI

IF YOU CROSS ME ONCE

ANGEL I II

IN THE BLINK OF AN EYE

By **Anthony Fields**

THE LIFE OF A HOOD STAR

By Ca$h & Rashia Wilson

THE STREETS WILL NEVER CLOSE I II III

By K'ajji

CREAM I II

THE STREETS WILL TALK

By Yolanda Moore

NIGHTMARES OF A HUSTLA I II III

By King Dream

CONCRETE KILLA I II III

VICIOUS LOYALTY I II

By Kingpen

HARD AND RUTHLESS I II

MOB TOWN 251

THE BILLIONAIRE BENTLEYS I II III

By Von Diesel

GHOST MOB

Stilloan Robinson

MOB TIES I II III IV V VI

By SayNoMore

BODYMORE MURDERLAND I II III

THE BIRTH OF A GANGSTER

By Delmont Player

FOR THE LOVE OF A BOSS

By C. D. Blue

MOBBED UP I II III IV

THE BRICK MAN I II III IV

THE COCAINE PRINCESS I II III IV V

By King Rio

KILLA KOUNTY I II III

By Khufu

MONEY GAME I II

By Smoove Dolla

A GANGSTA'S KARMA I II

By FLAME

KING OF THE TRENCHES I II

by **GHOST & TRANAY ADAMS**

QUEEN OF THE ZOO

By **Black Migo**

GRIMEY WAYS

By Ray Vinci

XMAS WITH AN ATL SHOOTER

By Ca$h & Destiny Skai

KING KILLA

By Vincent "Vitto" Holloway

BETRAYAL OF A THUG

By Fre$h

THE MURDER QUEENS

By Michael Gallon

TREAL LOVE

By Le'Monica Jackson

FOR THE LOVE OF BLOOD

By Jamel Mitchell

HOOD CONSIGLIERE

By Keese

PROTÉGÉ OF A LEGEND

By Corey Robinson

BOOKS BY LDP'S CEO, CA$H

TRUST IN NO MAN

TRUST IN NO MAN 2

TRUST IN NO MAN 3

BONDED BY BLOOD

SHORTY GOT A THUG

THUGS CRY

THUGS CRY 2

THUGS CRY 3

TRUST NO BITCH

TRUST NO BITCH 2

TRUST NO BITCH 3

TIL MY CASKET DROPS

RESTRAINING ORDER

RESTRAINING ORDER 2

IN LOVE WITH A CONVICT

LIFE OF A HOOD STAR

XMAS WITH AN ATL SHOOTER

CPSIA information can be obtained
at www.ICGtesting.com
Printed in the USA
LVHW042034220822
726558LV00007B/41

9 781958 111239